Someone

Bianca Harrison

Thank you, And Bless!

Bianca

www.authorbiancaharrison.com

https://twitter.com/mrsjanielle

instagram.com/mrsjanielle

https://facebook/authorbiancaharrison

~In loving memory of Elnora Turnipseed~

Susie Mae Pack "Teen"

My Grandmother: Who suffers from Alzheimer's and Dementia. I'm so glad you're here to share this experience with me. To God Be the Glory!

Love you dearly ~

Prologue

Camille

I awoke from a terrible dream. Sweat was dripping everywhere down my body, and my heart was racing. I kept seeing a face. It was a female's face that I recognized as the legendary Mary Stevenson. In the dream, she was tormenting me about her man, Taj Jabar, a well-known R&B artist.

I remember meeting Taj. He and I hit it off, and he invited me to an award show. At that same award show as he accepted his award on stage, he gave me a shout-out for, "wearing that sexy ass dress." Maybe that's how I even got onto Mary's radar in the first place—her man shouting me out with that comment.

I did make sure to look my best that night, not that I didn't all other times. But *that* night, I looked sexy as hell in a short silver sequined dress, silver studded heels, a matching clutch and accessories to match. My hair was done up nicely in a bun, and of course, my man on my arm. He belonged to me and only me.

I beamed on the red carpet prior to the event and sashayed as we entered. Who would've thought a shy girl all the way from North Carolina…now a city girl living in Atlanta… would be at an award show with other big-named celebrities like Mary J. Blige, Rhianna, Justin Timberlake, Kelly Rowland, Kanye, Sam Smith, Ne-Yo, Taylor Swift, and many more! This was a night I would remember for a long time to come.

I noticed that everywhere I went, Mary Stevenson followed me. She followed me from the photography booth, to the restroom, and the concession stand. *I didn't take her man*, I kept telling myself, *He came to me*.

I remember the night ending and flying back home to Atlanta, leaving Taj to get ready for another show the following morning. But when I looked on the internet, I was shocked. As I scanned through a few of the gossip sites from my smart phone, all the headlines read: *"Taj Dumps Camille, now back with Mary Stevenson."* Every site had some banner or comment across it; I became deranged from the thought of him using me to get back at Mary.

I jumped on the next flight back to L.A. and went straight to his hotel room. I didn't have a key so I lied to the front desk personnel about losing my key in the crowd. I entered the empty room and immediately began snooping through his belongings.

When I didn't find anything suspicious, I realized how crazy I was being, and decided to leave. I was losing my mind for nothing when I should just trust him. I made it to the door; but before I could make my escape, I heard voices of people coming into the room, so I hid.

I saw Taj and Mary making out as they entered the room. They moved from the couch, to the floor, then the bed. I managed to slip out without letting them know I was there.

As I made it into the hallway, I heard, "Camille...Camille!" I turned around to see Jennifer Lopez approaching. She saw the work I did for Mariah Carey's home on MTV Cribs, and wanted to know about my services. I hurriedly gave her my business card then apologized for being in a rush.

I escaped from everything. I just wanted out. I ran out into traffic, crying. I was distraught. I screamed so hard my chest pounded, I felt near a nervous breakdown, and in the process of my blind fury, I almost got hit by a car.

When I finally made my way back to the car I rented, I sat in the driver's seat in a daze. I was too weak to move from my spot. I wanted Mary to pay for the pain I was feeling, I needed to see her, ask her why.

Hours later I saw her exit the hotel and get into her car, and decided to follow her. My anxiety kicked in, and I flashed my lights several times to get her attention. She realized it was me trying to get her attention and pulled over to the side of the road.

When I made it to her car, "Roll the window down, Mary," I instructed her.

"Camille?" she said, with a look of confusion on her face. Nevertheless, she rolled her window down.

Without waiting for her to say anything, I yelled out, "Taj is mine!" You should have left him alone! All I wanted was a man of my own, why couldn't you respect that?" I asked her.

6

"Camille, you're crazy, you know that? I'm leaving!" she said. But before she could drive off, I reached in and stuck her multiple times with a pen I had. I pulled her out of the car, and continued to beat her until she couldn't move.

After I finished unleashing my assault on her, I got back in my car and left to catch the next flight back to Atlanta.

By the time I got home, my phone was ringing off the hook, but I wasn't ready to get into conversations with anybody, so I ignored all calls. A few hours later after I got settled in, I got on social media and read on both Twitter and Facebook that Mary was in a coma. The reports were claiming it was due to a carjacking. I smirked and thought, "The bitch had it coming!"

I let a few hours pass, and then called Taj. When he didn't answer, I thought it was strange because his morning show ended hours ago. When his voicemail picked up, I left him a voice message letting him know that I loved him.

Moments after leaving that message, I heard a noise outside. When I went to check it out, I was surprised to see that it was Taj coming to my door. I quickly ran to throw something on and took off my hair bonnet. I was shocked at his surprise visit. I ran to open the door to greet him, and was stopped in my tracks, when I realized there were cops everywhere.

You stupid bitch, you hurt my girl!" he yelled, shaking me. *"You crazy lunatic!"* he yelled, as he continued shaking me before a cop intervened. Another cop ran and pinned him down as I tried to come to grips with what he was yelling about.

As I woke up recalling my nightmare of a dream, my heart was racing. The dream was so vivid that my worst fear is that I'll be living this out in real life.

Chapter 1

Camille

Love can be painful at times! I stared at the ceiling and asked myself how long can I do this? I looked over at Greg and wondered, "Will he ever leave Michelle?" A man can fix his mouth to say anything when sex is involved. I've been waiting patiently for *it* —it being the birth of his baby with Michelle. He says he'll leave her after the baby is born.

As he slept, I stared at his amazing body; It's a damn shame that Greg is so mesmerizing. He has the tightest ass I've ever seen on a man. Not to mention, he can work wonders with his tongue. For a forty-year-old to have the body he does and know how to use every part of it is something else. He finally opened his eyes and looked around groggily and asked, "What time is it?"

"7:45."

"Oh shit!" Greg said sprouting from the bed.

"I didn't realize it was that late, I must have fallen asleep. Why didn't you wake me?"

I looked at him like *"really."* He kept going on and on about how Michelle, is probably waiting for him, and that he was supposed to be home around 7 p.m., and worried about what he was going to say once he got home.

"Let her wait dammit, I've waited long enough." I watched Greg get dressed, and then I got up from the bed and put my robe on. "The baby is coming any day now, right?"

"Yes..." he responded.

"So you might as well prepare her for your departure."

"Listen, Camille, you don't understand, it's complicated," he stuttered.

"Complicated my ass! I've been seeing and sleeping with you for over a year now. You're basically living two different lives, Greg. All these promises and all of a sudden, Michelle gets pregnant and our plans stall. I don't deserve this Greg!"

"Camille, listen, what we have is good. When things started out with us there were no strings attached. Then feelings got involved, and it only complicated things."

"Complicated? Complicated how, Greg?"

"You love me?"

"Yes."

"And that's just it. I love you too, but I need time to figure everything out once the baby is born. Right now I have to go. I'll call or text you later," he said, kissing me on my forehead before he left.

"Yeah...whatever!" I yelled behind his back. How in the hell did I end up in a relationship like this? *It's happening all over again*, I thought. Falling in love with a man that's not as committed to me as I am to him is not good. Yet I keep doing it. I allow them to lure me in, believing that they are committed. How can he tell me he loves me and not mean it?

I had put up a wall towards men, but then Greg happened, and I let my guard down just for him. Now I feel like he has screwed with my emotions. I hate that!

He comes over regularly. We chill, I fix him dinner, and we go out; we do everything couples do. But at the end of the day, he makes love to me and leaves. It's a messed up feeling when he leaves out my door to head home to another woman. I can't even explain the feeling; I just know that no woman should have to feel that.

Boy, love can be shitty! Why can't I have what I want, when I want it? Who's to say that when he goes through his divorce, Michelle will even cooperate? And how many more months will it take for it to be finalized?

I got up from my spot and walked over to my phone and noticed the light flashing on my answering machine. I hit the play button – beep, beep…"Camille, this is Nikki! Remember me? Your lovely friend who you seem to have forgotten about? I've been trying to reach you via phone, and email. Let a sista know you're okay; you've been MIA for days…call me."

After I deleted Nikki's message, I grabbed the phone off the receiver and dialed her number. She answered on the first ring.

"Dang, chic! Where the hell you been hiding at?" Nikki asked.

"Hello to you, too. I've been a little busy."

"Too busy to call your friend?"

"Well, I've been trying to figure things out and get my life back on track, that's all."

"So, what'd you come up with, Camille?"

"Nikki, you know my situation is complicated." I was trying to rush the call.

"Complicated, huh? Whatever, Camille. Are we talking about married Greg?" she shot back at me.

"Yes, and…?" I said, with attitude.

"*And* the fact that he is married and has been for years…and has a pregnant wife at home. Camille, do you actually think he'll leave her once the baby is born? That would be so cruel. Not to mention out of character, from everything you told me about him."

"I love him Nikki and he loves me."

"Ha-Ha, that's something they always say to get what they want, girl. Wise up…and you call me slow. You can't possibly be thinking about setting up house with this man, are you, Camille?" Nikki pushed for an answer.

"Nikki, why in the hell do you always have to be so harsh? Damn you!"

"Camille, all I'm doing is keeping it real with you. You're smart. We've been down this road before and where did it leave us?"

"I understand what you're saying, but you have to understand this is my soul mate, the man I was supposed to meet.

"Have you forgotten what happened two years ago with Walter, Camille?"

"Nikki, if I did forget, you just brought it back up."

"I don't want you to walk yourself down that path again."

After a moment of silence, I said, "Nikki, I have to go and take care of some business. Once I'm done I'll call you."

"Camille…Camille…" Nikki called out. I heard her, but before I knew it, I had placed the phone back on the receiver.

I headed into the kitchen to pour me a glass of wine – the perfect trick to calming my nerves. I then walked into the sitting area and scanned through the television, to find nothing on. Frustrated, I turned it off and headed for a warm bubble bath.

I turned on the water, added some silk midnight mimosa, and filled it to the rim. I dropped my robe on the floor, grabbed my glass of wine, then turned on my Maxwell CD and let him sing to me.

The water was warm and soothing, as I relaxed with my head laid back on the bath pillow. I reminisced about Greg filling me up in this hot tub last night. As my thoughts ran, they took me places I wasn't ready to go just yet, so instead I focused on something else.

I thought back to last night, while Greg was sleeping. I sneaked and inserted a tiny chip inside his phone, so I could monitor his calls. He probably will never know it's there.

I love him, but I don't want to be a fool in the process. I am going to hear every phone conversation he has. I'll know when he's talking to someone, and what he's telling Michelle. I'll be able to tell once and for all whether or not his intentions toward me have been true.

This is going to be interesting, I thought.

But once I gathered enough information, what will I do? Leave his trifling ass alone? Keep screwing him? Go off the deep end? What? I had no answer to those questions and hoped it wouldn't have to come to any of that, because my ultimate goal has always been to be with him.

I smiled, relaxed and drank my wine.

Chapter 2

Greg

Leaving Camille's house in Buckhead was awful…the traffic on Lenox was a mess. I couldn't believe she didn't wake me up. I hope she wasn't snooping around while I was asleep. It is something that she would do. What the hell did I even get myself caught up in? Just thinking about it made me realize that there are more than a few things she does that turn me off. Camille was starting to be a bit more clingy and needy.

I jumped on 85 towards 75 down the interstate. I put my Wale CD in the changer and bumped to the beat, while I tried to come up with an excuse to tell Michelle.

When I pulled in the garage, Michelle opened the door. "Honey, what happened? Dinner was ready over an hour ago; I called you twice and left a voicemail, did you not get my message?"

"Babe, the car had a flat. The wrecker came and took it over to the Tire Barn since the spare was no good; my phone was in the passenger seat on silent. I just now retrieved it from the seat, didn't even think to call home. I apologize, sweetheart. It's been one of those days," I said.

"Sorry to hear that babe, you had me so worried….you want to talk about it?"

"Not right now, maybe later. I just want to shower and get out of these clothes." I kissed her, then went to shower, changed clothes, and got ready for dinner. I didn't know if she believed me or not, I never snuck around or lied to her like I have been for several months now. In fact, I have no idea why I am doing it now.

I could tell once I came downstairs and sat at the table, Michelle was watching me. "Baby, what's wrong?"

"Greg, it's not like you to not call. What if I was in labor and this happened? Huh?"

"Baby, again, I apologize. I was trying to get the tire fixed head home, and then got stuck in traffic. You know this Atlanta traffic is a mess. If it helps I'll make it up to you."

Trying to get her to smile wasn't easy. "Don't let this happen again, Greg. You call at least ten times a day and forget this one time. It doesn't sound right, but in the meantime I'm going to accept your reason, and apology."

"Thank God! I could tell that you were not going to let that pass," I smiled. I played with her face, until she finally smiled back.

Michelle got up from the table, warmed my dinner, and sat back down at the table with me while I ate. My wife was gorgeous. I looked at her, nothing for makeup to cover up, no weave, nice body even during pregnancy, just flawless.

I couldn't get why I was seeing Camille…was it just for fun or to see how long I could get away with it? As much as I questioned myself, I couldn't find an answer as to why I was screwing another woman.

As I ate, Michelle and I discussed the baby's arrival. This would be our first child—and a boy at that! I couldn't be happier. The baby's room was prepared; my workload at the firm was going to be light for a couple of weeks, and Michelle and I had decided that we would rotate sleep schedules.

"A baby, what a bundle of joy," I said. "He is going to be so spoiled," I added.

"Of course, he will be a Langston," she giggled.

My phone vibrated on the table. *Shit*! I thought I took it up upstairs. I glanced at the text from Camille, asking me did I make it home safe. I quickly put the phone down and my heart started racing.

"Who's that?"

"No one. Just a reminder I set about a meeting I have first thing in the morning."

"Well, you're home now."

"With that said, Mrs. Langston, why don't you let me put you to bed. I'm done with dinner and want to make love to my lovely wife," I teased.

"Well, I do love pleasing my man," she said, with a sly grin.

I followed her upstairs and laid her down gently on the bed. I undressed her with my mouth, she was heated and demanded what she wanted me to do to her! I loved the way she talked dirty to me – it turned me on! She immediately suggest we switch positions as she sat up and put her juicy lips over the tip of my dick, I watched her slide it in and out of her mouth. It was hot and wet and sloppy, but it felt so right. As I moaned, I knew I wanted to be inside her juices. "Baby, you going to mess up my flow, pulling on it like that," I said. Michelle was a great lover and I returned the favor.

"Baby, I need you to climb on top of me."

"Are we trying to go into labor tonight?" she asked.

I smiled at her. With her stomach as big as it was, my wife still found a way to make love to me.

As she climbed on top of me, she sat her wet vagina on my face. Boy, was I in heaven! A man's throne is his wife's pussy – something I like to call "ownership." I licked her clit, circled my tongue around the inside then out. I ate her good; she eased off of me and rode me one good time. I squeezed her ass as I rocked to her rhythm, making her cum. She oozed all over me, she moaned and groaned; I felt myself cumming. "Cum with me again, baby!" I moaned. "Ah, that's it!"

"I know I felt it, too."

As Michelle lay next to me in my arms, I thought about how I needed to end things with Camille; I was playing a risky game. One thing led to another and Camille wanted more, something I couldn't give her.

Maybe in another lifetime I could see us happening, but right now in the present, I don't see it. But it's my fault because I led her on. I do love her and have told her as much, but not like I love Michelle. Michelle, I'm *in love* with. She's my rock. I couldn't change that for any woman.

How would Camille feel when I broke the news to her? Would she threaten my family? Would she accept it and move on? Avoiding her wouldn't be the answer, so I won't. Besides, that's taking the easy way out. I had to figure this thing out and get my life back on track.

Chapter 3

Michelle

I woke up the following morning to the sound of rain and a cup of tea. It felt so good. As I watched Greg get ready for work, I couldn't help but think how lucky I was. I've been married to Greg for eight years and he always knows how to bring a smile to my face. But for some reason I had this strange feeling that he was lying last night about why he got home late. I wasn't buying that whole flat tire story. His reason for not returning my phone call didn't feel right.

"Sunshine…" he said, distracting my thoughts. "I'm about to leave for work. I'll see you this evening. Better yet, how about meeting me for lunch at our favorite spot, Bacchanalia?"

"That would work. I have to run a couple of errands and then off to my doctor's appointment."

"Oh, babe…we have a doctor's appointment today?"

"Don't worry. This one you don't have to come with me. But I'll meet you at Bacchanalia, around noon."

As soon as Greg left, the phone rang. "Hello?" No sound. "Hello?" I said again, but still no one said anything on the other end, so I hung up.

When I went into the den to open the blinds, I noticed a black Lexus driving by slowly; it stopped for a second and then resumed its pace.

I figured that maybe whoever it was might be looking for someone or a particular address in the neighborhood, so I didn't think much of it.

I went upstairs to shower, and while I was getting undressed there was a sharp pain in my abdomen. I was thirty-seven weeks with only three more to go. I panicked a little, but was praying and hoping that it was nothing, and that the baby would hold off for a couple more weeks.

By the time I got out of the shower, I felt better, like it was just what I needed.

After I was dressed, I stopped to look in the mirror; I thought I looked damn good for a pregnant woman. I glanced at the clock, and saw that the time was nearing for me to get going. I set the house alarm and headed for my car. Outside, I saw my neighbor Brenda watering her plants, and waved to her as I got in the car and took off.

I arrived at the doctor's office, and waited patiently for my name to be called. Once I heard, "Michelle Langston," from one of the nurses, I followed her back to a room where she checked my blood pressure and weight. Before long, Dr. Smith arrived. "Hey Michelle, how are you and the baby doing?"

"I actually feel good," I answered. "But I did have slight pain this morning. It's been on and off for a few days," I confessed.

"Okay, well let's take a look," he said, as the nurse came back in. After lubricating my stomach, he began to investigate. Finally, he put my mind at ease. "Michelle, everything looks good. The baby's heart beat is normal and your uterus is where it should be at thirty-seven weeks. Your cervix has thinned out just a little," he said. "Most likely you were having Braxton-Hicks contractions, but your cervix has dilated one and a half centimeters."

"Huh? So what happens next?"

"Well, you are thirty-seven weeks with three more weeks to go and so far the baby is six pounds and healthy. He may come early, which can be any day now, or he may come just when he's supposed to. I want you to monitor and time your contractions; if they get worse, come to the office or go straight to the hospital. Other than that, you may schedule an appointment for next week, or we just may see each other sooner," he smiled.

As I was at the front desk scheduling my next appointment, my cell phone vibrated.

"Hello?"

"Hey, baby, are you still at the doctor's office?"

"I'm actually leaving now."

"Okay. How did everything go?"

"Everything went well. I was having some pain this morning and Dr. Smith said they were Braxton-Hicks contractions, but now I know why."

"Why?" he asked, concerned.

"Because apparently, our little one is trying to announce his arrival—maybe a little early—and we've already dilated one and a half centimeters. Dr. Smith wants me to monitor and time the contractions as they come. Other than that, the baby is healthy and may be any day now."

"Geez, I guess last night must've helped! You know sex is really good for the baby; we need to keep having it every night," Greg teased.

"You're funny. Well, I'm wrapping things up and will meet you at Bacchanalia in twenty minutes. If you get there before me, please order me the norm."

"Sounds like a plan, I'll be there shortly."

"I love you."

"I love you, too, baby. See you in a bit."

For some reason I kept hearing a beep after hanging up with Greg. I arrived at the restaurant and noticed the same car in the parking area that drove by our house this morning. But then I shook it off because in this world just about everybody had the same car.

As soon as I was seated inside the restaurant, I saw Greg, and flagged him down.

"Hello, sweetheart," I said, as he reached in and kissed me.

"You look radiant."

"Thanks, you don't look too bad yourself," I said. "So, what should we order?"

"I'll have the norm; what about you?"

As I turned my head towards the bar, I noticed a woman with mid-length hair staring at me. I turned my head, hoping she would do the same, but every time I glanced up she was still looking—not just at me, but Greg as well. I decided to ignore her.

The waiter brought us bread, water, and tea; he took our orders – Greg ordered the Jamison Farm lamb and I ordered their wood grilled New York strip.

After the orders were placed, Greg excused himself to go to the restroom. I glanced over to the bar where the woman had been seated, but she was gone. I looked around for her and saw that she was headed towards the door.

From what I could see of her, she was very attractive. Just as she was leaving, Greg was also returning to the table, and I noticed that he stopped dead in his tracks and watched her as she walked by, which from the was odd from the look on his face, made me think that he was gawking at her.

I thought that was strange. I couldn't believe he was checking out a woman while I was with him! But I wasn't going to let it slide because I felt it was disrespectful. As soon as Greg returned to his seat, I asked, "Why did you stand in the middle of the aisle and look at that woman who just went out the door?"

"What woman, Michelle?"

"The woman right there in the black Lexus that's pulling off. Do you know her?"

"No, never seen her."

Maybe I was staring so hard as she was driving off that she decided to wave. "That was strange because this morning I saw the same exact car she's driving, ride slowly by our house and that woman stared at me the entire time she was at that bar. I didn't get a chance to see who was inside the car because of the dark tint, but whoever it was sped off down the street." I looked at Greg and he was sweating bullets, "Greg, are you okay?"

"Yes, Michelle, I just got hot all of a sudden."

Chapter 4

Nikki

Why can't Camille find a man that's available? Thinking about my conversation with her yesterday made me think she was up to something. When she put her all into a man and it doesn't work out the way it was planned, trouble followed.

Camille and I have been good friends for years, and I have probably been her only friend. I am the only one that knows her and her secret from that awful night of the accident two years ago.

After it all happened, Camille wanted a new start and all of a sudden jumped up and moved to Atlanta, leaving me and her past behind in North Carolina.

"Mrs. Nikki Martin," I turned around to Mike, my husband for a little over a year. "What are you thinking about?"

"I was actually thinking about Camille. I'm a little worried about her; she has been really distant lately."

"Is that so? Nikki, you know I don't really care for Camille. I've always said she was jealous of you, especially since we got married. She didn't want to see you with anyone because she has no one."

"Mike, show some sympathy. Her husband died; don't you remember me telling you that?"

"Yeah, and I wouldn't be surprised if she killed him with her messed up attitude and her drama!"

My eyes grew big like he knew something. Lord, why did he say that? I almost fell over the coffee table.

"Be careful."

"Mike, you knew how we met and she was opposed to me finding a man that way."

"What, on the internet?" he snapped. "Shoot. People meet on the internet all the time."

"What's that supposed to mean?"

"It's not her happiness, it's yours, Nikki. Stop allowing your life to revolve around her because, if that's the case, you will definitely be just like her, unhappy."

"Sorry, Mike. I know…I know. I am just trying to be there for her. Do you mind if I visit her for a couple days?"

"I guess you can go visit that slut you call a friend."

"Mike, don't say that!"

"Well, that's the truth; your so called bestie is insane. I'm glad she moved! Remember me telling you about her coming on to me, huh?"

"Yes, I forgot about that incident."

"You are one good friend to her, Nikki. I sure hope she is as true to you as you are to her."

He told me about the incident that happened right before Camille moved, but I put it out of my mind and never asked her about it. My friend for over fifteen years would come on to my husband? Why? Something I could never figure out.

I would be the last person she would want to mess with after knowing what really happened to Walter.

"Sweetheart, I know your heart and it's genuine. If you want to visit her, that's fine by me. I only ask that you not bring any of her drama and sluttiness back with you," he said, with a smile, before kissing me.

My love for Mike was amazing and getting the same from him in return was enough for me. I longed for the feeling of my man. When he licked my earlobe I quivered at his tongue, my vagina was already throbbing through my spandex.

He pulled my spandex down to my ankles. "Bend over," he instructed. "I'm about to get a quickie in," he smiled.

I did exactly as he asked, because I was ready to feel him. As he eased inside of me, I swore I was about to explode from the inside out. He pounded into me so hard that I found myself trying to keep up with his rhythm. But it didn't matter how much assault he unleashed on me, I wanted it. "Deeper!" I told him. I wanted to feel all of him. When he was inside me deep, he let out a moan that let me know that my pussy was feeling good to him. "Yeah, baby!" he moaned. After a few more strokes, he pulled out and took my ass.

I had never let a man inside that hole until Mike came into my life, and he loved it from behind. After five minutes of rolling my ass to his rhythm, he said. "Ahh baby, this right here, ewe, keep backing it up for me...I'm cummin', I'm cummin' baby!"

"Mike!" I called out and looked back at him. I was afraid he was about to release and I wasn't ready. When he let out a loud moan, I knew that was it. I shook my head. I was frustrated, and asked, "That's it? Dang, Mike, I didn't even get mine, you selfish bastard!

Mike looked at me in disbelief. I was heated while I felt his semen run down my leg. He finally stood up.

"Maybe next time, you'll cum a lil' faster!

Chapter 5

Camille

Shit! I ran right into Greg as I was leaving the restaurant and he stood dead in his tracks when he noticed me. I kept walking to keep from making eye contact.

The moment I arrived home, I rushed inside and fell right into the recliner.

I had so many thoughts running through my head; I couldn't believe him! He was out with his precious wife having lunch. I thought about how stunning she was; Michelle had expensive taste by the look of her attire. Not only that, but the thought of her granting Greg his divorce, but when?

As I listened to his conversation earlier from my phone talking to her at the doctor office, I knew where he was meeting her for lunch. I'm so glad I inserted that tiny micro-chip inside of his phone.

"So that bitch has dilated, finally! Any day now," I said to myself.

Greg looked too chummy with her as I watched them from the bar. He kissed her gently as he walked in and greeted her and that shit made me angry. This motherfucker better not be playing with my heart, I thought, as I gritted my teeth.

I was thinking about my conversation with Nikki yesterday. Thinking about my marriage to Walter, had been weighing me down ever since she and I hung up. It brought back memories of the car accident he died in as we were headed home from dinner. We were married for ten years and I loved him so much – I gave up everything to be with him. The good wife; I was taking care of his every need, but didn't get the same in return.

Weeks before the accident, I found out Walter wanted a divorce. He was leaving me for another woman, who he had been having an affair with for two years. He fathered her one year old son. I tried desperately to save my marriage, had no idea it was in trouble, his answer was he fell out of love with me and the affair "just happened." He finally told me the truth after lying to me for months about who she was; that she was just his sister's friend. She just kept popping up everywhere we went.

It was devastating to find out the truth about her son, that he was actually Walter's. It tore me apart, I couldn't have kids due to a hysterectomy years before, and couldn't understand why this was happening to me. I drifted into a depression. Nikki was always there for me. She got me out that state of mind, and was my only true and dear friend. One day I came to reality and decided to fight back. I figured if he was leaving me for a trick he barely knew, it would be over his dead body.

Thinking back to that particular Thursday afternoon, I called Walter and asked him if we could go to dinner and discuss the divorce agreement. I promised not to fight him on the divorce settlement. He agreed and offered to pick me up and drop me back off at home. Once he picked me up, the drive was awkward – we rode in silence the entire route to the restaurant. Arriving at the restaurant I knew this would be my last moment with Walter, a man I thought I would grow old with. We were seated in a corner table in the back of the restaurant. After the waiter brought us each a glass of wine and water, he gave us a minute to look over the menu.

Breaking the silence I asked Walter, "Why are you doing this? Did I deserve this?" I looked at him for answers. "I have been your rock and now you want to throw it all away."

"Camille, I am so sorry, I can't express it enough. I fell in love with her and we have a child."

I started crying, the child is what hurt me the most.

"Walter, you never gave me any signs that we had problems and you've been seeing her for two years, where the hell was I?"

"Camille, please calm down so that we can talk rationally."

The waiter returned for our order, I wasn't even hungry. When Walter ordered a salad, I told the waiter to just bring me what Walter was having.

Walter waited until the waiter walked off and then excused himself to the men's room. I remembered the bottle I placed in my purse before leaving the house; I pulled the syringe out and twisted the top off the bottle, and made sure no one was watching. I mixed a couple drops of morphine and codeine in with his wine and another drop in his water just in case he drank both. I used a butter knife to stir the glasses mixing the drugs in each of them just in time as Walter returned to the table.

Minutes later our salads arrived. Walter said I should continue living in the house; he would pay for alimony, and anything else I needed to smooth the process.

"Just have the agreement drawn up and send them over," I said, but thought that he must have forgotten about the half million dollar insurance policy we both had in place.

"I'm stuffed and ready to go now, but let's toast to our last evening together, Walter."

Walter looked confused. "Camille, let's just finish our wine so we can leave."

As we did, he paid the waiter, retrieved the car from valet, and off we went.

As we headed on the expressway, my thoughts got crazier and crazier. I wanted him dead for his cheating ways. I wanted him to feel the pain I was experiencing. I was scorned and ready to attack. Walter got off the expressway and took a familiar exit as a back way to get home. He was weaving while driving. I glanced at him a couple times and saw that he was sweating, and he looked sleepy.

Cars blew their horns at us, warning us to stay in our lane.

"Walter, do you want me to drive? You are weaving. Did you drink too much?"

"No, Camille, I had only one glass of wine, but all of a sudden I feel dizzy, sleepy and am having trouble breathing. We'll be home shortly. I can make it there."

Walter started speeding more than normal and weaving again. I asked him to slow down, I was scared. I turned my head toward him; he was falling asleep at the wheel. I screamed, "Walter!" He made a slight swerve into the other lane and BOOM!

I remember people running to the scene of the accident, I tried to lift my head but couldn't. When I finally opened my eyes, Nikki was right there. I had fractured ribs, broken teeth, a broken chin, a broken leg, and facial scarring. I couldn't open my mouth to speak, and Nikki told me to keep it closed. Finally, I tried to ask what happened and to find out where Walter was, but Nikki told me to try to relax. All of a sudden Nikki completely looked away; I had tubes everywhere, my body was in pain, and I could barely talk.

"Nikki...where is Walter?" I asked, but nothing seems to come out, but Nikki knew what I was getting at.

"Camille, you and Walter were in a terrible car accident," she kept saying in between sniffs, "Walter is gone...dead...they couldn't save him," she blurted.

"WHAT!" I screamed in agony. What seemed to not come out, but tried to, due to the pain I was in, were the words "he can't be." I kept saying those words to myself, and then finally the doctor came in to confirm the news. After that I stared off into space.

After Walter's funeral, I had to fax the death certificate to our insurance agency in order to get the half a million dollar policy, because he was still my husband. But I did not worry about that until after my recovery. I was in therapy for weeks, due to the fractures in my leg.

How perfectly my plan had worked, I thought. He definitely didn't deserve me. I will do something nice for his son when I'm healed. I will give his girlfriend and their son my house so that the boy will have somewhere to stay and I will leave to start fresh. I just didn't know where quite yet.

Chapter 6

Camille

The phone rang and startled me – *who in the hell is this interrupting my thoughts?* I mumbled as I looked at the caller and picked up the phone.

"Yes, Greg..."

"Hello to you, too, Camille. What the hell were you doing at Bacchanalia today?"

"Damn, I can't have lunch? This is a free country and I have no ring on my finger. I eat where I want to eat," I said. The question is why you were there with your precious wife?

"I'm sorry. You just caught me by surprise and startled me, that's all."

"I noticed and that was the reason I kept walking. So, what was up with the lunch date?"

"Camille, she's still my wife, and I still have an obligation to her until after the baby."

"Really Greg?" I said, trying to understand his intentions. "You wouldn't be playing any games with me Greg now would you?"

" Calm down," he said. "No one's playing games, Camille. Michelle is emotional and needs me right now; we haven't spent any time out together, so she wanted to get out and have lunch."

"What kind of fool do you take me for, Greg?"

"What are you talking about?"

"Nothing…absolutely nothing," I said. "It is what it is."

"Camille, can I at least come over so we can talk about this some more?"

"Fine," I said, and then hung up on his ass. I heard his entire conversation with Michelle on the phone and then he lies to me? He's got balls! Men with money, power, good looks, and good dick think they can get away with anything. Let Greg keep fucking with me, I'll have to show his ass. I'm not that BITCH.

Chapter 7

Greg

Being smart is something I'm crafty at, so why am I doing dumb shit? Why am I risking my family fooling around with Camille? I asked myself this question over and over again.

Camille does have some worthy attributes. She is tall, slender built, beautiful, smart, funny, and rough around the edges at times. However, even with all that, she wasn't my wife, and doesn't hold the same qualities as my wife. Michelle is in a category all her own.

I met Camille a year ago at Starbucks. I was finishing up paperwork for a client when all of a sudden this woman invited herself over to my table and sat down.

"A man should never dine alone."

"I'm not alone. You see all this paperwork, lady?" was my response.

But she didn't care. While I was completely distracted, Camille sat and began telling me about herself – how she just moved to Atlanta and was an interior decorator, and about how she had just met with a client prior to spotting me.

I told her I was indeed married, and she told me she was a widow. We engaged in small talk, and before I knew it, she had me laughing. That's how it was the entire time she was there.

I kept my personal life at a minimum. We exchanged cards, for the sake of it, and then after a while, she dismissed herself and left.

A couple of days later, I received a call from Camille inviting me to lunch at her home, saying that she wanted to thank me for allowing her to invade my space.

I made every attempt to reject her offer because I knew going to her house was a bad idea, but she was persistent. I finally gave in and agreed to meet her.

After that day, one thing led to another and I've been screwing around with her ever since.

Now how do I get myself out of this mess without hurting her feelings? She's been making remarks and demands about me leaving my wife and that scares the hell out of me because it will never happen.

It was because of her demands about marriage, that I felt the need to go to her house. I really didn't want to go, but the sound in her voice when she called gave me chills.

I arrived at her home, pulled in her driveway and got out, just as her front door opened.

"Hey," she said nonchalantly.

"Hello, Miss," I responded, as I entered.

I walked in, with her close behind, then she grabbed me by my suit tail. I turned around to face her, noticing her eyes were red like she'd been crying.

"Camille, what's going on?" I asked, while watching her closely. "You sounded really upset over the phone. What's going on?"

"Greg, it's you...I don't know if I can wait until the baby is born, I want you to myself now."

"Camille you know I can't give you that!"

Camille was starting to play mind games. The shit I don't like, nor have time for.

She stepped closer, leaned in and kissed me, then unzipped my pants. She pulled my pants and briefs down to my ankles, and started massaging my balls. She finally knelt down, put her mouth over my dick, and sucked me hard, while gripping my ass.

Damn, I had to admit it felt so good when she did what she did. But after a while it was beginning to feel more like pain than pleasure, and I didn't come over here for this shit. I pulled back trying to get her to back off.

Camille was fucking me with her mouth, I started to grab her hair but as I looked down, she was staring straight at me. I wanted her to stop, but she began to suck, bite, suck, and bite as a routine.

"Camille! Dammit, that shit hurts!" I yelled at her.

"Cum, Greg, and I'll release you" she demanded.

"I can't cum when I'm in pain!"

She finally released me and stood up from her position. I could tell she was disappointed by my outburst. If I wasn't sure then I was certainly sure when she told me I could leave now.

"Camille, my dick is bleeding and I'm not going anywhere until you tell me what the hell is going on with you!"

"Greg, I just wanted you to stay focused, you looked tense when you walked in."

She left to get a washcloth and returned with twenty-one questions. "Greg, do you love her?"

"Her...as in Michelle, my wife?" I said, looking confused by her question.

"Yes, Michelle who else?"

"Yes, Camille, she's my wife for heaven's sakes. I love Michelle and always will; she is going to be the mother of my child," I said, trying to end the conversation and leave.

"I see. So where do I fit in, Greg? Huh? Can you answer that? I am your wife. I've been basically doing her job! You gave me hopes for us, and this is not a game, not to me!" she exclaimed, while pacing the floor waiting on an answer.

"Camille, please calm down." Then realizing just how far gone she was I knew it was time to tell the truth. "I had no intention of this becoming more than what it is. I meant what I said – that I do care for you and love you, but right now that's all it can be, I'm sorry." I apologize that I may have given you false hope.

As I moved closer to comfort her, she shot me a look I had never seen before. There was evil in her look; it was as though she had split personalities.

"Greg, you said you were leaving her once the baby was born. You've been fucking me for months, playing with my feelings, and to top it off, you say you love me, please! That's bullshit and you know it!"

I tried to reason with her. "Camille, right now let's just chill. Let's take a moment to think everything out. I need time. Michelle needs me right now. If I leave right after the baby, what does that say about me? I have an obligation to fulfill," I said, without holding back. This was becoming draining.

"Obligation! Screw you, Greg. You have no clue what obligation means. I will tell you this, if I'm not happy, no one will be happy. You come here every day and lay up with me and think everything is good? Greg, I do love you and always will."

Then I watched as she suddenly calmed down. And when she finally spoke again, I knew something was off. "But like you just said, let's chill. You obviously need time and so do I!" she yelled.

As I studied Camille, she seemed crazier than ever. I would have never thought that, but now with her threats, and comments, I'm starting to believe it. *"If I'm not happy, no one will be happy."* What the hell did she even mean by that? I wondered.

As I left, I noticed Camille looking out her window as I sped off.

I dialed Ed, my partner and co-owner of Langston & Hayes Associates, as I headed back to the office. I told Ed about having lunch with Michelle and running into Camille there.

"I thought you were ending things with her man, what's up?"

"Ed, man, Michelle said Camille stared at her the entire time we were eating lunch. She said that she saw the same exact car ride by the crib this morning, driving slowly through the neighborhood."

"You think that was just a coincidence, Greg that she was at the same spot as you and Michelle? You have no clue what you're dealing with; she has problems and is about to cause problems for you. Didn't I tell you what looks good isn't always good man?"

"Yeah, man, let me tell you the worst part. I went over there to talk to her. The first thing she did was unzip my pants. But then she did some crazy shit, man."

"What?"

"Man, she bit my dick until it bled."

"What the hell!" Ed screamed through the phone and started laughing like hell.

"That's not funny! She's psycho and had the nerve to threaten me." In the middle of talking to Ed, my other line rang. "Ed, man, hold on, this is Michelle."

"Hey, babe. What's up?"

"Hurry home, my water just broke."

"I'm on my way. Just sit tight. I'll be there in a couple of minutes."

I switched back to let Ed know what was going on and had to get to the hospital.

"Call once you get there," Ed instructed. "I'll let everyone know at the office and I'll meet you there later," he said, ending the call.

Before I pushed the end button, I noticed that my phone had bad static on the line. I heard a beep that would sound every minute, like a bad connection.

Chapter 8

Michelle

Waiting for Greg was like waiting on the dead. I had to remind myself to breathe in and out. I was home for nearly two hours and all of a sudden the pain started coming back to back. I timed the contractions; they were way too bad to be Braxton-Hicks contractions at five minutes apart. When I went to use the bathroom that's when my water broke.

"I can't have this baby at home," I said, as I paced back and forth through the kitchen.

I'd already called my doctor, and his office said he would meet us at the hospital.

Greg finally came running through the door. "Michelle, where are the bags?" he asked, calmly.

"They're over there, by the sofa. Also grab some towels and I'll meet you at the car. Don't forget to set the alarm."

"Wait for me, Michelle. I want to put the towels down in the seat before you get in."

"I'm in labor and you're worried about this damn car – it's going to get wet regardless, you have leather seats. Hurry let's go," I said. I was in too much pain to worry about some damn seats.

"Baby, I didn't mean it like that."

"Greg, hurry!" I said, breathing heavier than normal. I'm hurting bad. They're now three minutes apart."

The pain was killing me! But I did well, before I knew it, we had arrived at Memorial Hospital, and a nurse was there to help me into a wheelchair. A short while later I was in labor and delivery.

Greg was in and out, giving updates to our parents. The doctor came in and checked me; he said I was dilated to seven centimeters. I asked for an epidural to ease the pain, but was told that it was too late since I was dilated over five centimeters. I kept thinking to myself how these young mothers have three to five kids…it's awful. When it was time to deliver, Greg and my mom came into the room. Both of them held my hands as I pushed. The stronger the pains, the more I pushed. I remembered trying to scream because the baby wouldn't come out. Finally, after the last push, Dr. Smith grabbed my son's head as he entered the world. My mom squeezed my hand and smiled.

Post delivery, my body was sore, but looking at Greg made me forget that for just a moment. "Baby, you did it," he said, with a tear in his eye. I could tell that he was in the moment. He was a proud papa.

Our baby boy, Greg Jr., was a healthy 7 pounds, 5 ounces, and 19 inches long.

The nurses moved me to a room and the rest of the family followed along, and visitors came in and out. Greg talked to the baby and smiled at the same time, and then his cell phone rang. "Michelle, this is Ed, can you take the baby for a moment while I tell him the news?"

When Greg had to leave to talk to Ed, he was about to hand me the baby, but instead, Margie his mother stepped in. "This is my first grandbaby," she smiled, as she reached for him. "So you know he'll be spoiled."

As Greg talked outside the room, I heard commotion. My mother heard it, too, and she looked out the door. She pulled the door open and saw Greg talking to a lady who held a basket full of baby items. "Greg, what's going on," my mom called out. No sooner than my mom asked the question, there was a loud cracking sound. According to my mom, the woman had thrown the basket on the floor and walked away.

Greg finally walked back in with a worried and puzzled look on his face.

"What was that about, Greg?" I asked. We were all curious.

"It was nothing. Some woman wanted to drop off a gift claiming her sister's name was also Michelle Langston, and that she hadn't seen her in years. Don't worry; I alerted the nurse's station that the woman had the wrong Michelle. I told them you don't have a sister."

I looked at Greg, and could tell he was nervous. He was sweating and his phone kept ringing. It was ringing back to back, and I was starting to feel something was up. I then figured that maybe people were calling to congratulate him on being a first time dad. After a while, he finally put the phone on vibrate.

The nurse came in to confirm that I would be breastfeeding, offering to show me the proper way to do it. Everyone left the room, except Greg. She indicated that if all went well, maybe I could go home tomorrow; she left paperwork for us to fill out. She said she would be back in shortly to take the baby for his circumcision and baby pictures.

"Michelle, thank you for a beautiful son," Greg said with tears in his eyes. "I just want you to know that the two of you are my world. I love you."

"Greg, I love you, too. We're a team."

His facial expression turned sour. He looked like he wanted to tell me something, but then again maybe he was just happy.

Once the baby was fed, there was a voice and a knock on the door, and Greg jumped.

"Come in." It was Ed and a couple of co-workers, then walked in Dianne, my best friend since college. Greg and I agreed that Ed and Dianne would be the baby's godparents; they were honored when we asked them several months ago. Dianne surprised me; she had originally said it would be tomorrow before she could get here.

Everyone was excited about the baby. There were so many gifts I didn't know which gift came from who. It was all very exciting, but I didn't realize just how tired I was until Greg took the baby from my arms and, I felt myself dozing off; even with a room full of people.

As the day was coming to an end people started to leave one by one. I was so happy, but exhausted at the same time.

Finally morning approached and a doctor and nurse came in. After looking over my chart, it was determined that since all was well, I should be discharged by noon.

After we got the okay from the doctor on when I would go home, Greg headed home to shower, and stop by the office.

A little while after he had left, a volunteer from the nurse's station brought in a basket meant for me, and left it on the table next to the bed. I reached over and grabbed the card that was next to the basket and read it.

"Congratulations, Michelle, on the birth of your son, Greg Jr. Wishing you both the best. I wished it was me instead of you. You're a lucky woman, but so am I. One day it will be me giving birth...sooner than you think. Keep your family close." (CY)

"What the hell?" I thought, "Who was this person? This person had to know me, she knew my baby's name was Greg Jr. and why did Greg lie?"

This wasn't just any deranged woman looking for her sister with the same name as me. It just didn't add up. I put the card in my purse and looked at the items in the basket, it just didn't feel right. It didn't make any sense. I guess if Greg won't tell me the truth, I'll find out myself.

Chapter 9

Nikki

I loved working from home; it was one advantage of being the boss. I had been staring at the screen for hours and my eyes were tired, so I decided I needed a break. Mike was out supposedly looking for a job, he couldn't keep one for nothing. I needed him to be able to hold things down if I couldn't handle it or got sick, but I kept telling myself, "love conquers all."

The phone stopped my thought process; I looked at it and was surprised it was Camille. "Hey, lady," I picked up and said.

"You're in a good mood," she responded.

"Just surprised you called back. You know how you can get at times, but I planned on calling you back anyway."

"Oh, really?" Camille said acting surprised.

"Yes, I am taking a couple of days off to come visit…if that's cool with you?"

"Nikki, that's sweet, but I got too much going on right now. Can you hold off for a couple of weeks?"

"Camille, what is the problem? I want to see my best friend. You are in Atlanta, alone, and I miss you. We haven't seen each other in awhile," I whined.

"Let me get myself together before you come. I am a mess."

"Whatever, you better hurry up because I'm coming whether you like it or not. I feel like you've been hiding a lot of shit from me and don't want me to know what the hell you're up to," I laughed.

"Nikki, shut the hell up. You're always jumping to conclusions, as usual," she said, getting defensive.

"Camille, I'm sorry but since your involvement with Greg, you've shut me out. You're in Atlanta sleeping with this married man, not working much with all the potential you have. I know you still have a lump sum of cash to hold you down for awhile, but do something constructive with your time." I advised.

"Nikki, sweetheart..." Mike called out, interrupting my conversation. I turned around and looked at him, he gazed right back at me. "I didn't hear you come in."

"That's because your ear is glued to the phone."

"Nikki, see you don't have time for me," Camille said on the other end. "Mike controls you, listen to him in the background, has he found a job yet?" Camille asks.

"No," I said while he was staring at me.

"What is it?" I asked him. "I'm on the phone."

"Who are you talking to?" He asked.

"Camille," I answered, hoping he would leave the room.

Mike didn't want me to be friends with Camille – he never liked her. She is so misunderstood. It makes me wonder if he lied about her coming on to him.

"Camille?! Shit! I'm hungry! She'll have to wait, sweetheart!"

"Nikki, call me later and handle your lightweight because I don't have time to deal with your ignorant husband. He is such an asshole. I warned you about him. We'll talk later…" Click! Camille hung up.

I was so heated with him, and before I knew it I went off. "When you get a j-o-b and buy groceries in this house, then you can talk about food! Until then? Starve!"

SMACK! That's when his hand went across my face. "Don't you talk to me like that, I am the man of this house!" he yelled. "Dammit, I have been looking for a job. But you? You yap your mouth with that bitch on the phone and ignore me!"

"Did you just hit me? With all the shit I do for you, pay all the bills and take care of your lazy ass? I am the breadwinner because you can't keep a job!" I yelled. "Damn you," I yelled walking away.

"Yeah, I hit you, Nikki, and what are you going to do, hit me back? Shit, you weren't working when I came in!"

"Mike, go to hell!" I yelled from the hallway.

He followed behind me, and tried to grab my arm to apologize. "Look, I'm sorry. I had a bad morning, it won't happen again. I love you and all that you do for me," he said, trying to sound sincere.

I jerked away from him, walked into the bedroom and closed the door behind me. I was so naïve when it came to men, who was I kidding? Mike didn't love me. He was using me and he knew I loved him too much to kick him out. All I wanted was a man to love and treasure me. I held my pillow tight and cried.

I got up and went to my desk, wiping my tears. Mike kept knocking on the door with the same line, "Baby, please forgive me, I didn't mean it." Blah…blah…blah…I ignored his ass.

Moments later I heard the front door shut and his truck pull out the garage.

I went to the kitchen and grabbed a bottle of water from the fridge. As I walked back to my office, I picked up two pieces of paper off the carpet, which must have fallen out of Mike's pocket. One was a receipt and the other was a note that said, *Call me. 803-245-7109. I got something for you. Jose*

Who was Jose and what did he have for Mike? I thought. Hopefully, it was someone who was helping his ass get a job. I knew when I met him online he wasn't shit. He claimed to have so much but didn't have a pot to piss in.

But the time I spent chatting with him made me feel whole, like there was hope after all. It wasn't that he was a bad guy – just lazy, and not worth a damn in the bedroom, but I keep him around anyway.

I asked myself constantly, if love was blind. It seemed as though most women, including myself, just wanted a man who would love them unconditionally.

But, maybe that was too much to ask for.

Chapter 10

Camille

I called Greg and left him several messages; I really hoped he was not ignoring me. Michelle should be home from the hospital by now, with our soon-to-be "son" in tow. I thought about the idea of motherhood and smiled. She had no clue what was in store for her and how Greg was going to leave her for me!

I didn't want to take matters into my own hands, but if I didn't hear from Greg soon, he would leave me no choice. He cannot make a promise to me and then not keep it. We waited too long for this moment.

My cell phone vibrated, interrupting my thoughts. It was a blocked call; normally I don't answer, but felt the need to.

"Hello."

"Camille, this is Greg."

"Greg, why are you calling me from a blocked number?"

"My cell phone died and I didn't get a chance to call you back after receiving your text messages. Are you okay?"

"Yes I am, I just missed you that's all. Hoping you would come over later," I said, trying to smooth things over.

"Camille, you can't be serious after pulling that stunt and showing up at the hospital like you did. Besides, I don't think that's a good idea. Honestly, I have a lot going on and need to clear my head," he said, shooting me down.

"Is that my problem? No," I answered for him. "I came to the hospital to lend support, but you acted like you didn't even know me. You can make this easier on the both of us and do what you planned to do prior to the baby coming," I said angrily.

"Camille, I'm not *supposed* to do anything. And why are you threatening me? I'm trying to be cordial, but that shit you pulled was not cool. I have a wife and son who need me. You bring your ass to the hospital with a gift basket for whom? How did you even know we would be at the hospital?" he snapped.

"Motherfucker, I need you and right now you are pissing me off. What am I supposed to do Greg, huh? I love you; don't you see what it's doing to me? Making me into a person that's not me," I pleaded with him.

"I'm sorry for getting us both into a difficult situation... The feeling *was* mutual. I had feelings for you, but now I'm turned off by the things you're doing," he said.

"Had?" I interrupted.

"Camille, yes…lately they have been fading. I do care about your feelings, but that's all they are…*feelings*. This is really too much for me right now. I think we need to just chill out. I really have to go, so I'll talk to you later," he said, attempting to get away. But I stopped him before he hung up.

"Like hell you will! You have some nerve, Greg. You treat me like shit and talk about chilling out...you think I'm going to jump on your terms? You're going to come over here, I really miss you!"

"Listen, I really have to go," he said nervously, before hanging up.

I felt tears streaming down my face. I started pacing back and forth. When I had gathered my composure, I put on my shoes, grabbed my car keys, and headed out the door.

* * *

I drove like a mad woman and pulled over in a shopping center. I stopped at a hair store in Midtown, purchased two blond wigs, a red wig, makeup, and rubber gloves. The next stop was a thrift store off of Old National. I went in and purchased a few hand-me-downs. I left the store and then sat in my car contemplating my next move before heading home.

Once I arrived home I dialed the number to a van I saw for sale. After a few negotiations, the seller sold it to me for $1,000, but it had to be picked up that day.

I quickly changed into some of the clothes I picked up at the thrift store, covered myself in make-up, and threw on the red wig. I walked up the street and waited on the cab I called.

Everything was going according to plan, even though I looked like a homeless tore down hooker. The cab arrived, I had him drop me off at a shopping center around the corner from where the van was parked, and then I walked to my destination.

The owner was at the car lot waiting for me. Once it was confirmed that there were no problems, I paid the gentleman in cash, retrieved the keys and he handed me the receipt, then drove off. I could care less about a title.

I was trying not to leave any tracks behind as I tried to figure out a way to get the van in my garage without anyone noticing it. Once I got it in the garage, I spray painted stripes on the van; once it dries I plan to cover it to be on the safe side. I went inside to take off that hot ass wig. I looked in the mirror and didn't recognize myself. It's amazing what clothes, makeup, and some hair will do to your image.

I threw the wig and other items into the fireplace and burned them. Heading upstairs to shower, I felt lightheaded. Maybe this situation with Greg was getting to me.

I finally ate and laid in bed and was thinking about calling Nikki, when my phone rang, and it happened to be her.

"Hi, girl," Nikki quickly spoke.

"What's going on with you, chic?"

"You're in a good mood, Camille. You haven't sounded like this in a while."

"Whatever…" I laughed.

"Well, I was calling to see if you wouldn't mind me coming to visit you..."

"Nikki, you're more than welcome to come to Hotlanta! Besides, I miss my friend," I said, in a sneaky kind of way.

"Let me hang up and call you back to make sure I'm talking to the right person," she said, laughing.

"Just hurry up and get here, before I change my mind," I said to her, as we disconnected the line.

My mind was in overdrive, as I thought about how good it would be to incorporate Nikki into my plan. Greg wouldn't know what hit him after it was all said and done.

I decided not to contact Greg for awhile. I figured I would just let him think I was chilling like he said we would do.

He'll be back sooner than he thinks.

I went to my closet, pulled out a box full of video discs inside. "I think Michelle needs to know what her faithful husband has been up to lately," I said, smiling to myself.

Chapter 11

Greg

Camille is fucking delirious. I guess the saying Bell Biv Devoe, once said, "Never trust a big butt and a smile," is true. Camille had the audacity to show up at the hospital and then call like nothing happened.

I dialed Ed and waited for the phone to ring, "What's good, my man?"

"Man, you wouldn't believe the shit Camille pulled at the hospital! The bitch is crazy!"

"What do you mean at the hospital? I was there? Didn't we already figure the solution to your problem?"

"Before you got there, she showed up with a gift basket. I stopped her ass in the hall outside Michelle's room. If I wasn't there, there is no telling what may have happened."

"What! Man, she is trying to screw you over. How did she know y'all were at the hospital? She has some screws loose. You need to stop entertaining her altogether." Ed responded.

"You're right, bruh. I love my family and getting involved with her was the worst thing I've ever done. Nothing will make me leave Michelle; I fucked up."

"We live and learn. Not saying you're a smart cheater, but you had never cheated on Michelle before. You let your ego and curiosity to be with another woman other than your wife, get to you. I do believe that some females take your kindness for weakness and you fit the bill, you see how easy it was for you to hit that?"

"Yeah, you're right."

"Do you even know anything about her? Because it sounds like she needs to be in a mental institution."

Damn, talking to Ed made me realize I didn't know anything about Camille, which made me wonder more. But really, I just wanted to let it go and move on.

"To be honest, I know nothing about her, and at this point it doesn't matter. That's the past and now I'm moving forward," I added.

"I love you, man, I just hope everything blows over and she doesn't do anything else stupid."

"Yeah me too."

"Just stay focused and cheer up. It will work out for the best. I'm really happy for you," Ed said, toward the end of his call. "Kiss my godson for me when you get home."

"Will do, man! And Michelle is already planning the christening. I'll let you know the details."

"Cool! Talk later," Ed said as he hung up.

* * *

I was finally home, and was watching my two favorite people, Michelle and Greg Jr., as they slept peacefully.

I surprised Michelle with dinner: Tilapia, steamed vegetables, brown rice, and dinner rolls.

Michelle woke up to the smell of food and smiled as she walked downstairs. She kissed me on the forehead and gave me a big hug.

"Babe, I missed you."

"I missed you, too, sweetheart." Aside from that, I want to talk to you."

"About?"

"Work. I know you like your job, and you make a very good salary, but with the firm and my salary, you know I can hold it down. I would love for you to stay home with the baby. Then maybe later, we can have more children," I suggested.

"Greg, that's my career…"

"Baby, all I'm saying is consider staying home until Greg is three years old, I don't want him in a daycare."

Michelle broke out, "Three years and possibly more kids? We have your mom, who would love to keep him," she responded, with a smile.

"Yeah, but I want him here and you can still do a little consulting from home," I reminded her.

"Baby, I will definitely have to think about this. I love my job and having my own money. You know how independent I am…"

"Well, baby, you don't have to be independent with me. I know you want to think about it, but I hope you decide to let me take care of you for a change."

As soon as we both sat, the baby decided he wanted to join us as he awoke from his nap. I let Michelle go ahead and eat dinner, while I retrieved the baby.

After we had eaten, the doorbell rang. As I approached the door, I could hear people talking, and opened the door to find, Joe and Brenda, our neighbors, with baby gifts.

"Give me that baby," Brenda teased, as she hugged Michelle, who finally handed over the baby.

"He is so precious, with the cutest smile. You know we are just next door…if you ever need a sitter, just holler," Brenda said.

"We really appreciate the gifts…they are nice," I said to Brenda and Joe.

"No problem," Joe responded.

"Would you guys like any dinner?" I asked. "I just cooked."

"No thanks," Joe responds. "We ate not too long ago. We just wanted to see the new addition. I actually need to go rest I'm very tired."

"I hear you, I'm about to wind down myself," I responded.

"If you need anything, we are just next door," Brenda reiterated.

"We appreciate that," Michelle said.

As we said our goodbyes, Ed called to ask if I could fly out to D.C. on Sunday for a day trip regarding the Michael Malone child molestation trial coming up.

This case was very important and Ed was already in Boston, wrapping up another case.

I asked Michelle if it would be okay to leave her for a day, even though I hated to leave her and Greg for that amount of time alone. She insisted I go and get back.

"Greg, besides, someone has to work since you want me to stay at home remember."

I let Ed know I would be able to take the trip to D.C., and he already had a plane ticket for 8:45 that morning, which was one less thing I had to worry about on my end.

After cleaning the kitchen, and putting the baby down, we both showered and decided to watch a movie. Times like these were priceless, with those who mattered. Michelle squeezed me tighter as we watched "Love Jones." I thought about how we haven't done this in awhile as I held her.

Michelle glanced at me only to move in and kiss me gently. Minutes into the movie, Michelle was out like a light.

Chapter 12

Michelle

I am so grateful to have a wonderful husband like Greg, and now a precious baby boy. I was still debating about possibly staying at home full time. My college degree I worked so hard for will be no good if I decide to quit working, even if it's only temporarily, I thought.

Dianne called me and stated she would be in town this weekend to visit. I thought it was perfect, since Greg would be in D.C. She was the perfect godmother for my son.

My cell phone buzzed in my purse before me realizing it; it was Greg.

"Hey, babe," I said, answering the call.

"Just calling to check on you two."

"So far so good."

"I am going to finish up here at work and I will be home shortly to take over so that you can have a break."

I just smiled like a school girl and said, "Okay." Although, shortly sometimes turned into hours with Greg's work load.

We said our goodbyes and hung up. I noticed the card from the hospital sticking out of my purse. I pulled it out and read it over and over again trying to make out the initials CY, which still puzzled me. I really wanted to ask Greg about it, but felt like I needed to dig deeper and find out more information for myself first, in case he is lying about something. Maybe I am reading too much into it, but something just didn't feel right about it.

I looked out the window and saw Brenda raking her leaves. I was still thinking about the card. I logged onto my laptop and Googled the initials in the Atlanta area, but there were so many options. Plus, there was no way I was going to know who the card belonged to and it hit me, maybe I can get a print from the card to see who it actually belongs to.

I called a courier to pick up and drop the card off at a local company to have the prints checked out and traced, then have it sent back to me in a couple hours before Greg got home.

An hour went by, I got a call from the lab pertaining to the card, but they found no prints on it aside from mine. The courier was on his way to return the card back to me, as well as the information they found. When the courier dropped the card back off, before putting the card back in my purse, a thought rushed to my mind.

I reread the card again not understanding why someone was telling me to keep my family close as if they wished they were in my position. My first instinct was that Greg was having an affair; it seemed really strange especially when I think back to how he was acting in the hospital room after arguing with the deranged woman.

"Not my Greg," I thought. He has no reason to cheat on me, but I couldn't shake the thought for some odd reason. I hated to, but felt like I needed to do some investigation of my own to put my mind at ease.

I would start with his phone records; they will help me or at least give me a start. I figured I would call every number on the list and narrow it down to the time of day and how much interaction he has with his clients.

He's an attorney for heaven's sake, I mumbled to myself. He gets calls all during the day and night. Geez, this has to be worth a try. I didn't like snooping. What if I find something I really didn't want to know? How would I handle it if I do find something?

I went to our AT&T account and retrieved all phone records. I pulled up each bill for the last six months and checked each phone call. I printed them out and studied them before putting them in a safe place until I actually had time to go through them and start calling. I heard the baby on the monitor. Greg Jr. was fidgety. I put everything away and went in to pick him up since it was time for his feeding.

An hour later, Greg walks in with Chinese food.

Once I finished eating, I went upstairs to shower. Moments later, I was back down with the family. I noticed Greg talking and cuddling with the baby and they looked so peaceful, it was priceless.

I was consumed with so many thoughts I started to worry, but kept telling myself I have nothing to worry about.

Greg noticed me staring, so he got up with the baby and kissed me trying to show me some love since he said I was jealous of the love and attention he was giving the baby. I smiled because this was my family and I'll be damned if someone comes in trying to destroy what we have! MY INVESTMENT, MY FAMILY!

Chapter 13

Nikki

After confirming and printing out my ticket to Atlanta, I felt such a relief knowing I would get a much needed break. After working nonstop and landing a major contract for my firm, this trip was right on time I thought, until I saw Mike.

"Hey beautiful."

"Hi, sweetheart, how did the interview go?" I asked him.

"The interview went really well, they will get back with me in a couple days if I'm hired."

"Cool."

I reminded him of my upcoming trip to visit Camille. He had the nerve to ask me if I had cash so that he could get groceries and gas to get by until I got back. I went to my purse and gave him the Visa card, so that he could get out of my face.

"Thanks, babe, I'm headed back out to fill up the truck and stop by the store, see you in a few."

This is really starting to get to me, little does he know that Visa only has $150 dollars on it, it's just a Visa card that you can keep applying money. Mike will never have access to my account.

Mike is lazy! I don't believe he ever went to an interview. He kept pressuring me to add him to my account. I may be a fool to put up with his bullshit, but not that damn foolish. I make all the money and pay all the bills; every time he gets a job, he finds a reason to quit. There is always an excuse.

I heard a noise coming from the kitchen and realized Mike forgot his cell phone. I picked it up and read the text that came through, *"Have you left yet? I can't wait to see you".*

What the hell, I thought. I quickly jotted down the number as I heard Mike's truck pull back in the driveway. This text didn't come off as business to me and I was curious who was behind it.

Mike ran back in the house to get his phone, and went back out the door, got back in his truck, and drove off. I was dying to see who the text belonged to, so I threw on a pair of jeans and a t-shirt, grabbed my keys, and drove to the nearest pay phone that still existed.

I pulled out the piece of paper and noticed the card that I found on the rug earlier which had a Jose name written on it which belonged to the same individual's number on the paper. I dialed the number and after a couple rings the person picked up.

"Hello?"

"May I speak with Jose, please?"

"Yes this is he, how may I help you?" he said, with an accent.

"Hi, Jose. My name is Nikki. I found your number and multiple texts from you in Mike's phone and want to know what's going on?" I asked.

"Nikki, me and Mike are just friends, are you his ex-wife?"

"No, I'm actually his wife! What is your connection with him?"

"What do you mean his wife? Mike is divorced..."

"I don't remember getting a divorce! Mike lied to you! What is going on between you and Mike, Jose?" I said, yelling at him through the phone.

"Nikki, do you mind if we meet later?" he asked.

"About what?"

"Mike," he said.

I agreed to meet him at Brew It Up, a coffee shop in town off of 4th and 5th around 7:30 p.m.

Hours later, Mike came rolling in. Never in my life have I known a person who takes hours to fill up a gas tank and go grocery shopping, only to come back with four plastic bags. I may be naïve, but I am not as stupid as he may think I am.

"Mike, it took you almost two hours to go to the grocery store?" I asked.

"What now, woman!" he said.

"Nothing, just...nothing. I'm going back to the store. I got up to look in the bags and found nothing but junk food. I thought you bought some food for the house. There's nothing but junk food in here!"

"You need some money?" he asked, with a smirk on his face, like he had something to offer me.

"How the hell you gonna ask me do I need some of my own money?" I said, giving him a stern look.

"Now it's *your* money?" he said.

"Yes, dammit. I work for it!" I grabbed my keys, walked out the door.

* * *

Thirty minutes later, I arrived at the coffee shop. I sat in my car until I saw a guy that fit Jose's description. He walked into the coffee shop. Bingo! I adjusted the wig I had on. I quickly got out and headed towards the entrance of the coffee shop.

I purchased a latte and approached the guy I assumed to be Jose, sitting in the corner. I extended my hand to him, and sat down. "Nice to meet you, although, I'm very curious to know why you wanted to meet."

"Nikki, to be honest, Mike and I have been having an affair for months now."

"What?! Are you shitting me?" I said in anger. "You're having an affair with my husband?" I asked Jose. I looked around the coffee shop in rage at what this man just told me. "Divorce, affair, divorce, affair…with another man at that, this has to be some kind of sick joke."

"No, I wanted to meet with you because he told me you two were divorced. He said that the settlement requires him half of the house you both share, which is why he hasn't moved out."

"What!"

"Yes, that's what Mike told me, so I just rode with the flow of things. I trusted him because I never had a reason to question him," Jose said.

"Well, I'll be damned, that bastard! He's been living in my house for free; paying no bills and now he's having an affair—with a man!"

"Yes, you're the only woman he's ever been with. Look, I don't want to cause problems, but I wanted to get to the bottom of this, just as well as you do."

Now I was really pissed! It took all of me not to break down right in front of him, but I held it together. I was so distraught and here I thought Mike was trying to get it together.

"What about protection? I have to know, Jose."

"We never use it. He said he hasn't slept with you in months and once we fell in love the condoms came off," Jose said.

I felt bile creep up in my throat. I shook my head in disbelief, the thought of us just having sex over the couch and then Jose telling me he was with him earlier just brought me to tears.

Jose apologized but I asked him not to say anything to Mike about us getting together; he should continue to act as though nothing happened. I would deal with this situation when I returned from Camille's. Jose agreed we should kick his ass, but I have something better in mind. This man has jeopardized my life, now it's time for me to do the same in return.

Chapter 14

Camille

All that beating and hammering was getting on my nerves! I hired a couple of guys to come over and build me a false wall inside of my closet, which will also be sound proof.

I hoped they would be finished soon; they have been working on it all day.

It was hard listening to Greg's calls and especially those with that damn Ed; he made me out to be a nut case. Greg really let me know how he felt; it was very interesting because I knew his whereabouts and what was going on in his life.

Knowing all that helped me put my plan into action because no one screws over Camille. I'm sure Walter learned his lesson now that he's six feet under. For some reason I knew dealing with Greg was too good to be true. Men like him only care about themselves and don't care who they hurt in the process.

I went through the attic to make sure I had enough baby items for Greg Jr.'s arrival. Once the guys were done with the closet, I plan to move all items there. I couldn't help but think how good of a mom I plan to be to my soon to be son. I heard my name being called as I quickly emerged to meet the gentlemen in the bedroom, who quickly gave me an overview of the wall they constructed together. I was very impressed. I retrieved the key that had a tiny opening to the closet and then sent the guys on their way.

I headed to the kitchen in hopes of fixing myself a relaxing drink, and then I noticed the flash on my phone, which indicated Greg was talking to someone.

I clicked the button on my phone and listened as I heard Greg telling Ed that he hadn't heard from me in awhile, that he hoped he got through to me because I was getting too attached. Ed responded by telling Greg he may have dodged a bullet dealing with me, but a woman like me always resurfaces, and for Greg to leave the past in the past and have a safe flight to D.C. I smiled at the fact that Greg thought he could get rid of me that easily.

"So, that's what he thinks, huh? I got something for him sooner than he thinks," I muttered.

Ending the call, I couldn't help but think I might need to make my move while he's out of town; it would be perfect timing. Pacing back and forth, I needed to make sure I had all my ducks in order, including running a few errands before picking up Nikki. I realized, after this weekend I will have a son – my son! Since Greg ruined my life in hopes of us being together and one day starting our own family, even if I had to adopt, it's time to give him a dose of his own medicine.

* * *

I ran my last minute errands, dropped everything back off at home, and made sure everything was in place for Nikki's arrival. I hesitated in changing again before picking her up but decided to keep on my casual attire. I had to hurry to the bus station; Nikki would arrive any minute now.

Nikki's bus pulled up as I parked. I got out and motioned for her, she walked toward me and we fell into each other's arms like old times.

"Nikki, you lost a lot of weight, you look great!" I teased.

"Stress will do it," Nikki responded.

"Stress, oh never mind…we'll talk about it at dinner."

We headed over to the Atlanta Fish Market, Nikki's favorite restaurant whenever she was in town. We talked nonstop during the ride, catching up. Once we arrived at the restaurant and got seated, Nikki told me about Mike; his laziness, which was nothing new to me, and his affair with another man.

"Nikki! That's foul! You've given him everything, he contributes nothing! How much more will you take of his bullshit?"

She looked at me, dazed, until the waiter came over and took our orders. She shook her head in disbelief and I wasted no time in telling her about my relationship with Greg and his manipulation, and that my payback is right around the corner.

"Camille, what do you have in mind?" Nikki whispered.

"Nikki, you'll see tomorrow. He'll be out of town," I told her, while looking around the restaurant.

"How do you know he will be out of town if you haven't talked to him, Camille?"

"Damn, Nikki, you ask too many questions!" I explained to her the chip I had inserted into his phone while he slept.

"What the hell, you've been listening to his conversations?"

"Shhh! Keep it down, Nikki, and yes that was my only way to get the truth from him," I said defending myself.

"Camille, that's low. Although, I don't agree with what you did, it was a smart idea," Nikki said as she laughed.

I couldn't let Nikki know my plans, for fear of her freaking out and asking too many damn questions.

Once we left the restaurant, we stopped by the store and got our favorite snacks. We left from there and arrived at my house, where I led Nikki to the room she'd stay in during her visit. I went downstairs to fix us both dirty martinis and popcorn while we had a little girl time before it got crazy. Nikki was very surprised with the décor of my home; "Not bad, huh?"

"Girl, you have really outdone yourself this time. Your skills are on point," Nikki said while she admired my work of art.

Nikki and I got comfortable, watched a few movies, ate all types of junk food, and got tipsy. Nikki told me about all that's been going on with her and Mike and I told her what she needed to know about me and Greg. I realized Nikki and I are alike in many ways: our lives are both complicated by looking for happiness in all the wrong places with the wrong men.

I finally confided in Nikki about the time Mike tried coming on to me, which led to her vase getting broke. She realized that Mike had lied to her about the entire incident. I felt like I was trying to protect her and her marriage at the time, a reason why I never said anything. At that moment we shared a few laughs and tears, until we decided to call it a night.

The next morning I woke up with a headache, Nikki came into the bedroom jumped on the bed like a kid, and asked about the van parked in the garage. I looked at her and told her it was part of the plan. "Since you're here, you can assist," I joked, but was really serious.

"Camille, what the hell is going on and what are you getting me into?"

"Nikki it's not bad, calm down, just fun and games. I'm using it to scare Michelle," I said trying to make light of the situation.

Nikki wasn't sure and hesitated at first, but I had to assure her so she would follow through. Once Nikki left the room, I picked up my phone and listened as Greg talked with Michelle, who was home alone with the baby. He was finally in D.C. and called to let her know he got there safely. I thought this was the perfect time to put my plan into action. Boy, I couldn't wait to see how long it would be before Greg came running back to me.

Chapter 15

Greg

Washington, D.C. felt more like winter; it was very windy even though the sun was out. I couldn't wait to wrap up things and get back to Michelle and the baby. It felt good talking to Michelle and knowing Dianne arrived early, so Michelle wasn't alone. Michelle insisted I stay for the night, but I planned on leaving right after the meeting with the prosecutors. I gave Michelle a list of all the emergency numbers in case she may need me.

I felt a whole lot better since I hadn't heard from Camille in a very long time, and hoped it stayed that way. I don't need any drama in my life. I love my family and the baby brought a new perspective in my life.

I adjusted the mirrors in the rental car and drove deep in thought for fifteen minutes to The Jefferson Convention Center.

Meeting Clifford and the others was perfect timing. The charge that took place in D.C. has been getting a lot of media coverage and bringing Langston & Hayes on board would be good for the firm. While Ed was in Boston wrapping up another trial, he faxed over the additional paperwork needed to proceed with this case.

Going into the meeting, we went over details surrounding the Michael Malone case, a former principal who was accused of molesting seven kids of both genders and killing two of his victims. This is a case in which we sought the death penalty. Michael was also connected to numerous cases outside the area and would be tried on those cases, as well. As I thought about this case, it changed my perspective on things since I now have a child of my own.

Clifford was a great attorney and had never lost a case; he was also featured in several magazines such as Fast Company, Black Enterprise, and Consumer Business Report. His credibility was awesome. Ed met Clifford at a conference three years ago and had been in contact ever since. Clifford promised to one day work with him.

Wrapping up on what should have been a short and sweet meeting turned into the longest meeting ever. We all met at the hotel for cocktails shortly after the meeting, while all the men discussed their personal lives I tried to back away from the conversation. Clifford was on wife number three and couldn't seem to keep his pants up; he wanted to screw every female he came into contact with. I must admit I was tipsy to be talking about my own situation with Camille to the fellas. They all waved their hands in laughter like they do it all the time and teasing me as a first time cheater. I focused the conversation on Michelle and how compatible we are, which meant no need for dipping with a wife like her, Clifford grinned a big grin.

"Boy, who you fooling? You're in love now because of the baby. Your ass be fucking Camille in your sleep!" Clifford shouted and grinned again.

"No, no, no…it's not like that. That situation is over," I responded.

"Yeah, whatever…it ain't over until she says it's over. Remember Camille has a pussy, she holds all the cards," Mark hollered from the table and laughed out loud. I was ashamed to be at the same table with these guys and here I thought they were professional – they had me fooled.

I wrapped things up and told Clifford, Mark, and Donald I had to bounce to catch my flight in time, running before I have to answer any more questions by opening my big mouth.

"He's running, y'all; it got too hot in the kitchen," Donald said.

"Okay, damn, seriously I have to leave." I gave all the guys dap and went to pick up my car from valet. I staggered and could barely walk straight. I decided to take Michelle's advice and stay at the hotel for the night; I didn't want to get a DUI in D.C. I sat on a bench to call Michelle.

"Hey, you," Michelle said.

"Hey, babe. Meeting is over and I think I am going to take your advice and stay the night," I looked at my phone for a moment. "Baby, hold on," I heard several beeps and thought my other line was ringing but apparently not. I guess I had way too many drinks because I started hearing things.

"Sorry, babe, I thought someone was calling." I told Michelle about the meeting and having drinks with the fellas, which was the reason I couldn't make it home. I would have my car parked from valet and call to change my flight first thing in the morning. I heard the guys coming around the corner and told Michelle I had to go.

"Hey, Greg, you still here, man? I thought you'd be gone by now," Mark said, when he saw me on the bench.

"Yeah, don't think I'll be heading out as planned…too many drinks," I said.

"Well bring your ass with us. We're about to find a strip club," Mark said as all the fellas chimed in.

"No, thank you, I'll pass," I said.

"All right, but you have no idea what you'll be missing, pussy everywhere," they all teased and headed out.

I should have gone out as I thought about it. Clifford had a driver. Oh well, that means I need to stay in and get some rest. Although it was still early in the day, I could always go home later, but I wanted to check in and get some much needed rest.

My cell phone rang several times before I noticed it was ringing, but didn't recognize the number. I answered it anyway,

"Hello? Hello? Helloooo…" No one was on the other end, so I hung up. It rang again and it was the same thing. Heading to my room I couldn't help but think those calls came from Camille's crazy ass; I just hope she hasn't returned to causing problems for me or it will be hell to pay!

Chapter 16

Michelle

With Greg out of town it gave me some time with Dianne; she had been there for me through thick and thin. Dianne came in a day earlier than planned and I was glad to see her.

Dianne took the baby for a stroll around the neighborhood and then came in to announce they were taking a ride. I knew she was going to spoil the baby like her very own; he was very fidgety but the ride would put him to sleep. That was fine by me; I needed a couple minutes to myself.

I talked to Dianne about the situation with Greg and she gave me some insight although she kept it real with me and like always she supported me. I was wrong for snooping, but felt like I needed to go through the phone records; not sure if anything is there or not, but it's worth a try. The initials on the card had me puzzled and I needed to know whose they were.

Once Dianne left with the baby, I went through the phone records and noticed several numbers incoming and outgoing in the Buckhead area or at least that is where the number was listed. I highlighted every number that had multiple calls. Greg had a client record he kept with all contact information on all clients he represented. I needed to retrieve all the names and numbers, which were sorted by month and last names. I should have been a detective I thought. I could match the client names with the numbers, what didn't add up I would call.

I went to Greg's office and went through his files; he kept a file at work and home for legal purposes. I sat at his desk and went back to the month of March. I was able to match 17 out of the 21 numbers; this digging made me crazy, I thought, sweating and all. I ran upstairs to pull out the old prepaid phone I once had that I never threw out. The phone was intended for a co-worker's daughter, but her mom didn't want her to have a cell phone at the time – she was 10 years old. I thought all kids these days would love a phone at her age and never returned the phone back to the store.

Running through the house like a woman on a mission, I had to think fast before Dianne got back, what was I actually doing? Did I not trust my husband for God sake? I asked myself. I called the card that actually puts the minutes on the prepaid phone it came with when I bought the phone and quickly added 90 minutes to it; I also liked the fact that the phone isn't traceable. What the hell will I say when someone picks up?

I dialed the first number, it rang three times but it seemed like forever. My heart was beating fast in anticipation of someone picking up the phone, but it went to voicemail with the name Richard Gaines. I scratched that number and dialed the next one…rang twice…

"Hello," said the voice on the other end.

"Cathy Yates, please," I blurted.

"Sorry, you have the wrong number," the lady said on the other end.

"Ma'am, are you sure, this is the number I was given to locate Cathy?" I asked bluntly.

"Yes, I'm sure. This is Tonnie Yagle, ma'am," the lady said.

I proceeded to the next number. I felt like I was wasting time and energy. The third number I called rang several times. Just when I was about to end the call, I heard a woman answer.

"Hello?"

"May I speak with a Cathy Yates."

"Sorry, no Cathy Yates, you have the wrong number."

"Are you sure? Maybe I'm reading the package wrong, the initials are CY," I lied.

"Ma'am, you have the wrong number. My name is Camille Young." she responded.

"Oh, okay, Ms. Young, sorry to bother you." said before hanging up.

BINGO!

Satisfied that I'd found the person I was looking for, I put the phone away. There was no need to call any of the remaining numbers.

As I went back through all the past months, her number was listed on all of them throughout the day. I went to the computer and did a Google search on Camille Young and sure enough an address was listed for a Camille Young in Buckhead, Georgia.

I hurriedly called Troy, an investigator, who had done some work for my employer in the past to see if he could do an investigation. As soon as he had agreed, I quickly provided all payment information to him before Dianne made it into the house.

"Why are you sweating?" Dianne asked, as she entered the house.

"I was trying to clean before you guys got back. I'm about to jump in the shower," I lied.

"Girl, you just had a baby! You need to sit your behind down and rest. Go ahead and take your shower, I got this."

All I could think about while I was in the shower were all the lies. I wished Greg would just tell me the truth. There were too many red flags. First the commotion outside the hospital room, then the multiple calls on the phone records. Things just didn't feel right.

After I showered, I dressed in a pair of sweats, and a T-shirt, and headed downstairs to feed my little man.

I loved looking at my precious baby. He was a blessing. Just as Dianne headed upstairs to change into comfortable clothes, the doorbell rang.

I looked out the window before opening the door, and saw an unfamiliar white delivery van. "Who is it?"

"I have a flower delivery for a Michelle Langston," the woman responded.

When I opened the door, I was greeted by a woman holding a bouquet of flowers. She was an attractive brown-skinned woman, wearing lots of makeup, and a mole.

"Can you sign here, please?" she asked, handing me a clipboard.

I looked up at her as I was signing. "Can you tell me which company you work for—"

But before I could finish my sentence, she pushed past me. "What are you doing?! You need to leave!" I shouted.

By the time I saw the gun, it was too late and chaos ensued from there. She had the gun pointed directly at me. I was terrified, but my first thought was to grab my baby and make a run for it. I pleaded with the lady to take whatever she wanted, but just let me get my baby. She shook her head as in NO, I jetted as fast as I could knocking over everything in sight, but she was dead on my heels. "Dianne!" I screamed. But the jabbing in my shoulder cut off my cries for help.

"Dianne!" I continued to call out. She stabbed me again, this time in the leg. I tried struggling with her to get the knife away from her. I felt sharp pain all over my body. Dianne ran to the stairway and asked, "What's wrong?!" and ran downstairs.

"Dianne, the baby, get the baby!" I yelled. Dianne noticed the lady, as she ran towards the sleeper. She then pointed the gun at Dianne; she quickly made her way over to the sleeper and scooped my baby up, heading towards the door.

"Please don't take my baby! Please don't take him!" I pleaded with her, as I dragged myself to the door. Dianne grabbed the phone to call 911 and ran to the door to get a trace on the vehicle. Brenda heard the commotion from outside and ran over to help, while Dianne was screaming on the other end with the 911 operator. I was bleeding all over and screaming to the top of my lungs, "NOOOOO, NOOOOO! She's taking my baby!" I cried out.

Brenda ran back out the door to get a good description of the van. The lady ran with my baby in her arms and jumped in the van and sped off. I cried and cried, "This can't be happening!" I hollered as I cried, for my baby's safety and the pain I was enduring.

I went into a daze, hoping when I came back to reality this would all be a dream.

Chapter 17

Nikki

"Holy shit!"

Camille tricked the hell out of me! I sat in the van, watching as she ran toward the van with a baby dangling from her arms.

She pointed the gun at me, and yelled, "Nikki, drive dammit!"

I panicked. "What the hell have you done, Camille?!" I yelled.

"Nikki! Right now I need you to hush and drive! Go down two miles, turn right on Clemson, and there's an alley on the right. Turn there and park!" Camille was barking orders left and right.

I couldn't even think straight. The thought of what Camille might have done with that gun had me scared out of my mind. Not to mention, taking that woman's baby!

"Nikki straighten up and turn here!" she screamed. The baby was crying and too much was going on. I did what she said and turned the van into the alley. "Park behind my car!" she ordered.

"Oh my God! Is that why you left early this morning?! To drop your car off here?! Answer me, Camille!"

"Nikki, I'll explain everything once we get home," she said. "Right now, I need you to stop asking questions!"

"When we get home, Camille? I doubt if we even make it."

By that time I heard sirens all over the place, helicopters over buildings. She threw me clothes to change into; I did what she said. She had it all figured out – change clothes, change wigs, she even had a car seat for the baby in the back seat of her car. We hopped in the car and drove in silence, for what seemed like hours.

"Damn, Camille I didn't come to Atlanta to get mixed up in some bullshit." Camille didn't answer. She just drove in a daze without a word.

At that point I realized that she had this shit planned way before I got here and used me to be a part of it!

* * *

Finally back at the house, Camille went to the bathroom as I followed her with the baby. That's when she pulled out a bloody knife and the gun. "Oh my God," I said, as I jumped.

"Camille, what have you done? Did you hurt that lady?" My heart was racing and my eyes grew bigger, all this for a man, I thought. Now I was part of her crime.

"Nikki, calm the fuck down. The gun is not loaded; I used it to scare her, but ended up stabbing her by mistake so that explains the blood. She's alive, so don't panic," Camille said, in a rage.

I tried to make sense of what just happened and what she was telling me. "Camille, what are you going to do with this baby and a stolen baby at that?"

"Nikki, the baby is technically mine, she just birthed him. I'll decide when to give him back, *if* I give him back," Camille replied. "I got it all figured out, Nikki, so don't wrack your brain trying to figure out what I'm up to."

This bitch done lost her mind. Camille was crazier than I thought, and I don't know why I didn't see this coming with all the talks that led up to this.

I watched as she pulled the second wig off, and cleaned the knife. Then she started talking about how Greg betrayed her and all that has happened in her life this past year. She sounded like Greg owed her something. I was totally shocked at what just happened and what I was witnessing; this was not the Camille I knew.

"Camille, you need help…honestly, Camille, do you think Greg will come running back to you after what you just did? You just stabbed his wife and kidnapped their baby for heaven sakes!" I shouted, trying to get some sense into her.

Camille only looked at me with a blank stare as if she was about to have a break down.

I got up, paced back and forth. I was supposed to be on vacation enjoying time off with my best friend with no drama, away from Mike, now I find myself part of a crime I didn't commit.

"How could you drag me into this shit, Camille? Huh?" I shouted. "Camille, answer me!"

"Shhh…Nikki, turn up the Goddamn television," she hollered.

Oh my God! I couldn't believe what I was hearing on the news, there's a manhunt for two females and a sketch of the woman who kidnapped the baby.

Lord, have mercy! They found the van and they're collecting evidence that may lead to us. "I knew it!" I shouted. I started to panic.

"Nikki, we're good. There's nothing in the van that leads back to us; the van is not even registered in my name, nor is it insured, we were riding dirty! Ha Ha!"

Camille found it to be a laughing matter – it was all a joke to her.

"I bought the van for this purpose…with cash, so I assure you, we're good. Damn girl, loosen up," she kept saying.

I stayed glued to the television; it was some shit out of a scary movie. The news anchor reported that Michelle was in critical, but now stable condition. There were witnesses talking about what they saw. There was also a nanny or friend at the home at the time, and a neighbor, who both gave descriptions; I shook my head in disbelief. I looked over and watched Camille as she cradled the baby, who she called Greg.

Camille asked me to follow her upstairs. I did and what I saw puzzled me. She had a soundproof room designed just for this baby, a bassinet, formula, and clothes. Everything a mother would need to care for a baby. Her plan was definitely thought out. I was speechless and excused myself before I threw up!

Every time I glanced at the news, I wanted to cry. As mad as I was at Mike, I wanted to be home. Nothing compared to what I had gotten myself into, and I didn't want any part of it.

I went to Camille's bar and poured myself a shot of Patron. I don't normally drink, but I needed something to help take my mind off things. And it worked because not long after I took the shot, I could feel a burning sensation in my throat, that was working its way through my body, and making me forget the stunt Camille pulled.

I wanted to get out of the house, but feared what might happen to the baby if I left. I didn't need that on my conscience, so I stayed.

Camille came to comfort me. She knew it wasn't right and to get me involved was a big mistake.

Chapter 18

Camille

I turned my attention to the television and saw Greg appear. He looked good as he pleaded with the kidnappers. "Please don't harm my son. We just want him returned to us safely," he said into the cameras.

A reward was set for $10,000 for anyone to come forward with information that led to the solving of the kidnapping.

As I watched him, I could tell the incident had taken a toll on him; it looked as though he had been crying all day, and I could tell that he hadn't had any sleep. I couldn't believe I actually went through with my crazy plan, but now that it was done, there was no turning back now.

"I did this for us Greg. *For us.*" I said, talking to the TV screen.

Nikki walked in, looking like a ghost; we both watched the news together. With all that has happened I didn't bother to check my phone. The red light flashed letting me know Greg was en route and on a call.

I went upstairs to put the baby down, made sure all baby items were out of sight, just in case I was a suspect.

"Camille, your phone is flashing, it's Greg," Nikki called out.

When I answered, I listened as Greg filled his mother and aunt in on Michelle's condition. He stated she was stabbed four times…twice in the left shoulder, twice in the leg, and about the difficulty with getting the bleeding to stop. But he said that overall, her condition was stable.

"Oh, my God! Camille, you lying bastard! You said you stabbed her *by accident*! *Four times is not an accident*! You were trying to kill her!" Nikki shouted.

"Not now, Nikki, I'm trying to listen! I then over heard another conversation between Greg and Ed who then made accusations towards me. If only I could get my hands on that damn Ed, he would be one less problem to worry about! Honestly I believe that Greg was starting to believe Ed's accusation.

Nikki suggested that I call Greg out of concern, which I thought wasn't a bad idea. It would give me a reason to hear his voice.

I waited for awhile, then dialed Greg's number, which he answered on the first ring.

"Camille."

"Hi, Greg, I just saw the news and heard what happened. Sorry about your family. Is there anything I can do to help?"

"Thanks, Camille, but there's nothing you can do unless you know who did it."

"Sorry, who would want to do this? On a personal note Greg, was there another woman you were seeing besides me?" I asked him, just to see what he says.

"Are you fuckin' kidding me?! My son is missing and you're trying to confront me about another woman!"

Greg got very defensive as he tried to throw shade at me for asking him such a question. He went on and on about the possibility of someone knowing something. He was hurt, yet he was still on the other line trying to get me to break.

"Sounds like I struck a nerve and for the record Greg, I had nothing to do with your wife and son, please throw shade elsewhere!"

"I'm just trying to find out who is responsible, but if you have no information, I will talk to you later," and his phone went silent.

"Greg! Greg! Wait a damn minute!" I called out but no response.

"You see, Nikki, this is the bullshit I've been dealing with you see!" I yelled, because now I was angry.

"Camille, calm down, you have to understand Greg's situation. His son is missing and his wife has been attacked!"

"Nikki, it was so nice to hear his voice, though. I know he will come around; it's just not quick enough. I know I sound foolish, but he is what I need."

"No, Camille, you need Jesus!" Nikki said, with her smart ass.

* * *

Later in the evening the doorbell rang. I peeked out the window and what do you know it was Greg. Nikki and I looked at each other. Everything was out of sight; baby and all as Nikki headed up the stairway. I gathered myself together and answered the door.

"Greg, what are you doing here?"

"Hi, Camille, I needed to see you," he said, while looking around my place.

"So, what's up, you looking for something?"

"Nah, I just got a lot on my plate. My wife was attacked and my baby has been kidnapped. Dammit Camille, where were you when this happened?"

"Greg, I suggest you take your suspicions somewhere else. I can't believe you would suspect me; Greg! How dare you!" I said, trying to stay calm.

Greg apologized for coming off so strong, but he still wasn't being real with me. He stood in the middle of the room with his arms folded, staring at me, as if I was going to go off on him or something. Maybe that's what he was looking for but I remained calm.

I approached him with a hug, but he didn't respond back.

"I have to leave," he said moving away.

"Can't you just say a little while longer?" I asked him, as he turned on his heel.

He stepped back and said he had to leave and would talk to me later. I asked Greg to stay, but he didn't budge. He went out the door as I was on his heels.

"Greg, baby, what's going on? Talk to me. Greg…Greg…" I called out.

He got in his car and left. I stood in the doorway in tears and couldn't believe he just left me standing like that.

"What's your plan now? Why are you doing this, Camille?" Nikki came up behind me and asked.

"I don't have a plan, but one will surely be in place." He didn't leave Michelle as promised and now I have to take extreme measures. *After Walter's death, I vowed not to let another man treat me badly, and Greg is doing just that.*

Nikki was still standing behind me waiting on an answer I suppose.

"Greg has no clue about our son."

"Camille, listen to yourself! You said 'our son.' Nothing is yours."

"Like hell it's not, Nikki! Greg will find a way to work it out, I know he will. It's just a matter of time," I said trying to convince myself that he will.

Chapter 19

Greg

Something wasn't quite right with Camille. I had this strange feeling come over me. Her behavior wasn't normal and she acted like I was supposed to abandon Michelle for her crazy ass. All the signs were there and I never saw them until now. I kept wondering if she was behind all of this, and if she was, I will strangle that psychotic bitch!

I was praying non-stop that whoever took my son, was taking good care of him. This was all a nightmare. All I could think of was the baby's safety and Michelle's recovery. Arriving back at the hospital was a hassle. Everybody bombarded me with questions I didn't have answers to. Being known in the community had it perks, but this was not one of them.

"Hey, sweetheart," I said, as I walked into Michelle's hospital room.

"Greg, where is our son?" she asked, looking confused, but already knew what happened.

Everyone in the room was silent...Dianne, my mom, Susan, and other members of the family. I had no idea Michelle didn't remember the baby was taken during the attack.

I asked everyone to excuse us while I spoke with my wife. Once they left, I tried to explain to Michelle that the baby was kidnapped during the attack and that the community was out there looking for him as we speak.

"What!" she screamed.

I tried to calm Michelle down, but she was getting hysterical and needed the information to sink in. Michelle cried and cried, as I explained to her what happened. This was the worst feeling in the world, trying to be strong, when I wanted to break down myself. Suddenly two detectives walked in and asked to speak with Michelle and Dianne alone regarding the accident.

I went out into the waiting room and grabbed Dianne to answer the detective questions.

"Mrs. Langston, do you mind if we ask you a few questions regarding the accident, it won't take long?" one of the men asked.

"No, I don't mind," Michelle said, dryly.

"If you don't mind detectives I would like to sit in on the questioning," I said.

"No problem," Detective Ball responded by flashing his badge that displayed his name.

"Mrs. Langston, can you remember anything at all? Tell us what happened prior to the kidnapping, and please take your time," Detective Floyd said.

Michelle relayed the details of what happened the afternoon Greg Jr. was taken as she started to remember how the baby was kidnapped from our home. She seemed to remember it in vivid detail.

"Then what happened?" Detective Floyd asked.

Michelle said she turned around and that's when the lady pointed a gun in her face. Michelle ran to get the baby out the sleeper and called out for Dianne, who was upstairs at the time. The next thing Michelle remembered was a stabbing sensation. The lady had pulled out a knife and stabbed Michelle in the shoulder twice as Michelle tried to run for the baby. Michelle and the lady struggled, and the lady stabbed her with the knife again, this time in the leg.

Michelle started crying hysterically as she rehashed what happened.

Dianne spoke and gave her statement. She described the woman and the getaway van.

Michelle added the woman wore a blonde wig, lots of makeup, had brown skin, and a mole by her chin. In total shock, my eyes grew wider than a football field. I'll be damned if Camille didn't have a mole in the same location. That was something that couldn't be disguised.

Michelle just couldn't believe someone would do something like this. She got along with everyone, but it had to be someone that knew she was pregnant and wanted her baby because it seems like that's the only thing the kidnapper cared about.

Detective Floyd turned to me and asked, "Do you know of anyone who could have done this?"

"No detective."

The detectives said they would be in touch and were working the case around the clock. They handed me their cards and left.

Soon after, the doctor came in and gave us an update on Michelle. The doctor said that it's a possibility she could go home tomorrow or the day after depending on how well she did in the next twenty-four hours. Michelle was in so much distress and it was killing her that she wasn't out there looking for our son.

"Greg can you please bring back my laptop? At least I can go on every social networking site and bring everyone up to speed on my son's kidnapping," Michelle said.

"I'll stay here with Michelle while you help with the search," Dianne said.

"Thanks," I said. I need to head home and meet with the security company on an upgrade to our home system.

I walked over to kiss Michelle, assured her our baby was safe, and that lots of people were out there looking for him. She was so fragile I had to be careful what I said to her; however, I had to be strong for her sake.

* * *

After leaving the hospital, I went by the office to speak with Ed.

I waited until we were alone, and I told him my concerns about Camille and the visit from the detectives – Michelle's description of the attacker and the detective's questions. Ed thinks this was all Camille's doing. She found the perfect time to put her plan into action when she knew I was out of town. But how did she know that because I didn't tell her?

"Ed, man, I have a gut feeling she is behind this."

"I do, too, but we need proof," Ed said. "You know the procedure as an attorney, man."

"Yeah, I know," I said staring out of Ed's office window. "Man, if she has anything to do with this, there is no telling what I may do to her!"

Just then my phone rang, and I'll be damned it wasn't Camille. I showed Ed the Caller ID.

"Man, get rid of that broad, she's trouble."

I was so angry that I threw my phone across Ed's office, the only piece of device that connects me to Camille.

"Man, what the hell are you doing?" Ed yelled.

I was going crazy. I know a phone can be replaced, but at that moment seeing her name on my screen made me livid.

Ed walked over to pick my phone up from the floor. He had a puzzled look on his face. "What's this?" Ed asked, holding up a tiny chip that had fallen out the back end of my phone.

"It looks like a micro-chip, but where did it come from?"

"It came from your phone. It looks like you've been hacked!" Ed said, in disbelief.

I walked towards Ed and took the chip out of his hand and looked at it. I couldn't believe this shit!

"Ed, you know what this is?" I asked, like a dummy.

"Greg, I know exactly what that is and who did it, but why?"

"Camille, That sneaky bitch!" I screamed in agony.

She knew my every move, no wonder she just so happened to pop up at Bacchanalia, then the hospital and, Lord behold, my home.

I knew at that moment Camille knew where my son was. I had to be very careful at how I approach her going forward; she was now the key to getting my son back, safe.

"Greg, man, I hate to say this, but you need to come clean with Michelle and get the detectives involved to strategize a plan. First, we need to get a background check on her and you need to at least stay in contact with her to stay on her trail," Ed suggested.

"This is some bullshit, Ed, and you know that! How am I supposed to keep the press away? That would destroy my reputation, the company, and my marriage. These people are camped out everywhere looking for a story."

"What's more important, your reputation or your son?"

I slowly put my phone back together minus the chip and decided to follow Ed's advice and call Camille. When I reached her, she was so calm and acted so concerned, that it was getting the best of me. I decided to play along with her and tell her what she wanted to know. I promised her I'd stop by later and hung up.

"Greg, man, be careful. Michelle said the lady had a gun, I suggest you protect yourself," Ed said before walking out the office.

Chapter 20

Michelle

I tossed and turned all night from pain in my leg. Dianne paged the nurse to give me some more pain medication. I still couldn't understand why this happened.

The nurse came in with some pain reliever. After the nurse left, I thanked Dianne for being a really good friend and told her how I appreciated her being by my side during this whole ordeal.

"Would you call Greg so that he can give us an update on the search?"

I cried every time I thought about my child out there all alone and worried for his safety. I didn't want to think the worst, but that's what overloads my mind at times. I just pray whoever took him will not harm him. I didn't know what to think, I would lose it if they don't find him soon.

"Michelle, it's okay to cry. Please let it out. I feel your pain, but I have a feeling he'll be home soon," Dianne assured me.

* * *

Hours passed. I must have dozed off, but was awakened by the ringing of my cell phone.

I didn't recognize the number, but picked up anyway since it could be anyone regarding my child's kidnapping.

"May I speak with Michelle, please?"

"Speaking," I responded.

The caller was Troy, the investigator I called to investigate Camille Young prior to the attack.

"Michelle I've been following the news and heard about what happened to you and your baby's disappearance. I'm praying for you both. I know this is a very difficult time for you, but I have some information I want to share with you, which may be connected to the kidnapping."

I was speechless, but managed to tell Troy to proceed.

Troy went on the say he had a package that contained photos and personal information that he thought I needed to take a look at. He did state that the investigation was not around the clock because of his workload, but felt like what he did collect may be relevant. He didn't start the investigation until a few days ago. He would send a courier over to the hospital with the package shortly.

I was shaking with curiosity. I wanted to see what was inside the package, and requested that Troy deliver it as soon as possible. I asked that he address it to Dianne, so that she could pick it up and go through it if Greg just happened to be there asking questions.

"Thank you, Troy. I will contact you if I have any questions."

Dianne looked on as I explained to her about the call and the mysterious package Troy is sending over. I had to tell her my reasons for wanting to find out who this woman was and why, which didn't sit well with her, but after pulling the card out of my purse and looking at the initials, she, too, was curious.

Moments later, Greg walked in with roses. He came over and kissed me, then propped my pillow for me to sit up. He updated me on the search and on another news conference that was set up. He assured me that more people were joining the search team, looking in wooded areas, dumpsters, housing complexes, and everywhere else they could think of, but knows he's safe out there somewhere. I looked at him in tears as he turned his head away because he, too, was teary eyed and scared.

Dianne offered to join the search, but Greg asked her to stay with me since his mom and my parents were out looking as well.

We all were startled when the phone in the room rang, as Greg excused himself to the restroom; Dianne answered it and stated it was front desk with the package. I asked her to get the package and open it when she got to my house.

"Are you sure, Michelle?"

"Yes, I'm sure. I trust you. Also, when you get to the house, please bring my mail back with you," I said, laughing.

Greg walked out asking what we were whispering about.

"I have to stop by the house and your wife wants me to bring the mail back," Dianne said, covering for me.

"No worrying about bills in the hospital," Greg said.

"Hold on, Dianne," Greg said, digging into his wallet. He gave Dianne the new security code to the alarm and told her about the monitors in the foyer.

Dianne left with the information and I was alone with Greg for once. He walked over and hugged me, then got in bed behind me in a fetal position and held me. I laughed at the thought of the nurses coming in and seeing us like this. I held on tight and felt tears forming in my eyes.

"Greg, are there any past clients that might have been upset with you about a case or any enemies who might want to harm us?"

He took a deep breath and said, "No."

"I've been wracking my brain since this happened," he added.

The look on his face said otherwise, but for the moment I was going to take his word for it.

Greg jumped when he heard a knock outside the room. Both detectives walked in and gave us a run down on the van they found. They ran the VIN number and located the guy it belonged to, but the guy sold it days ago to a young lady who paid cash for it. So there was no trace of paper work, signature, tag, or insurance on the van. This was something that was planned and I seemed to be the intended target.

Detective Ball stated the guy was cooperating and may have footage of the woman paying for the van on camera, since his place had surveillance cameras and hopefully it will lead to something. As least it was a start.

Both Detectives Ball and Floyd stated they are working the case non-stop and that they would find my son. Greg walked the detectives out and I saw him talking to them outside the room.

The phone rang, and this time it made me jump.

"Michelle, is Greg in the room with you?" Dianne asked whispering on the other end.

"No, he's outside the room talking with the detectives, what's up?"

"Well I opened the package, But I'd rather you look at it for yourself."

"Dianne, what is it? Whatever it is it doesn't sound good," I whispered.

Dianne shared with me what was in the package pertaining to that of Camille Young. There were a few pictures of her and Greg together. She was a (either tall or petite) tall, petite, with a brown skin tone. The envelope contained information about where she lives and the car she drives which was a black Lexus. The pictures of her face weren't that clear. One of the pictures, she noted, was taken yesterday. It was of Greg leaving her house. I choked after she mentioned that piece of information. I was really confused.

"Michelle, are you still there?" Dianne called out.

"Yes, yes. I am just trying to consume all this information. So, Dianne, you mean to tell me Greg has been having an affair with this woman?"

"From the looks of these pictures and the information Troy provided, I'm afraid so, Michelle, but I can be wrong."

It took all of me not to get up and kill his ass. I was so distraught I didn't know what to do besides cry.

"Michelle, calm down. I knew I shouldn't have told you. I don't like this no more than you do. I can't believe this shit; I've known Greg for years and never would have thought this. I would rather you not say anything yet, you hear me, Michelle? Let's play it out and see if he comes clean first. Promise me you won't say anything?" Dianne asked of me.

I promised and hung up. The nerve of this bastard! "All these years I've invested, been nothing but good to him, and he does this to me?" I was in a rage.

I had to see these pictures for myself. I needed to see what she looked like and the nerve of that whore to show up at the hospital after I've given birth was foul.

I quickly wiped my face as I saw Greg entering the room looking crazy as ever. He assured me again this ordeal will be over soon and touched my hands; his touch was making me nauseous.

"Baby, what's wrong?" Greg asked, as I pulled back my hands.

"Nothing, I feel sick," I turned my head not wanting to look at him.

Greg's phone rang and supposedly it was Ed, he took the call while whispering and stated he needed to run some flyers by the office.

Like I believed that shit. I looked at him and said, "Go right ahead." I was not in the mood for more lies; it would soon come out. Dianne returned with a bag of goodies and the package, which was sticking out of her bag. I could tell she was also upset about the information she read based on her comments toward Greg.

Greg said he was running by the office and would return shortly to take me home; Dianne gave him a stern look, "Really, Greg!"

Chapter 21

Nikki

I kept looking at the phone and noticed no calls from Mike nor had he returned my calls. I called out to Camille who was singing lullabies to the baby like he was hers.

"Yes, Nikki?"

"I'm going to leave you for a couple days. I have to head home and handle my affairs."

"You mean Mike?" Camille responded, as she peeked in.

"Yes."

"Don't be a fool and open your mouth about what's going on here," Camille smirked, but was serious.

"Girl, please. This is your problem. I'll be back. I need to make sure that baby will be okay."

"Nikki, you don't have to come back. I'm good, there is no need for you to come back and check on me."

Before I could say anything else, she walked away. I went to call a cab instead of Camille dropping me off at the bus station and noticed a breast pump. "You've got to be kidding me!" I mumbled. Camille is a really sick individual.

It sank in that Camille used me all this time and put me in a situation that could have been deadly. I thought for a moment, did she really want my company when she said yes to me visiting her? She was only using me as her pawn. What kind of person does this to her friend? It brought tears to my eyes just thinking about it, but what Camille really needed was help. She was clearly unstable.

I was distracted by the horn of the cab. "Camille, I'm gone," I yelled.

She came out her room and walked me downstairs. "Camille, call if you need anything and from a prepaid phone," I said, because I had a bad feeling Greg was on to her.

"Nikki, please don't be worried. We'll be fine, but don't wait by the phone. We'll talk later," she said, as she rushed me off.

Just like that, I got in the cab and drove off.

Once on the bus, I had some time to think, especially about what happened with Camille and Mike. Both of them didn't mean me any good, so why can't I cut them off?

Hours later after a long ride I was finally off the bus and pulling up in my garage. "Home sweet home," I said. It felt really good to be here.

Mike was home, at least his truck was. This will be a surprise since he didn't know I was coming back so soon.

I walked in, dropped my luggage, took off my shoes, and rambled through all the mail. "Bills, Bills, and more Bills... what's new?" I thought.

I called Mike's name, but heard thumping and whispers instead and for some reason I had a funny feeling. I tip toed and walked closer to the bedroom and quietly turned the handle.

"Nikki, baby, what are you doing home so soon?" Mike asked in a calm tone while pulling up his drawers.

"Dammit, I live here, did you forget that shit? What the hell is going on? You have to close the door now to put clothes on?"

"No, I just walked in and probably shut the door behind me by mistake."

I looked at him and knew something was fishy, especially if he was home alone and had the bedroom door closed. I pushed the door as hard as it would go, hitting whoever was behind it.

Oh my God! I gasped. "What the hell is going on?" I asked, hysterically.

A voice came from behind the door. "Consiguió maldita!"

Finally the person emerged. "Jose, what the hell are you doing in my house?" I yelled.

I know I left town knowing that my man was sexing another man and raw doggin' it, but I didn't expect this shit in my own home either.

He looked at Mike and said, "Pensé que ella no viene hogar hasta el viernes, mentiroso!"

"Jose, you better speak English boy! No one understands that shit you talking about!" I said in a rage of anger and walked to my closet and opened my safe to retrieve my .32 caliber.

"What did you say Jose, Im'ma ask you one more time?" I said.

"No, I told Mike I thought you weren't coming home until Friday and called him a liar," he said, while trying to gather his clothes up.

"What the hell is going on? You two know each other?" Mike asked.

I pointed my gun at him in tears, asking Mike how he could do this to me. "Baby, I can explain. It's not what it looks like."

"Mike, get your shit and get out of my house…NOW!" I demanded.

Jose tried to explain while he was putting on his clothes that Mike lured him over to talk since he wasn't accepting his phone calls, so he went along with the plan we discussed. He tried to break it off and that's when it just happened. Mike looked dazed and confused trying to put two and two together as he kept asking what was going on.

I shot one time in the air and both men were scrambling trying to beat each other out the door. "Nikki, please let me explain," Mike pleaded.

"No need. I was on to your ass before I left to visit Camille. I met Jose, who agreed to go along with your game until I got back. See I'm not as slow as you think, Mike!" I said getting angry all over again.

I looked at Mike and couldn't believe he was gay, he kept saying he wasn't gay, but what do you call it when another man is fucking another man, idiot?! I went out the door firing more shots into the air. Mary, my next door neighbor ran over, and said she called the cops. She didn't know what was going on and saw why I was so pissed as she looked at Mike in disgust.

The police came in a hurry, people were standing outside; I walked back inside my house leaving Jose and Mike outside putting on their clothes.

An officer knocked on the door and asked what was going on. I quickly explained the situation and the gun shot in the air. The officer then checks my gun registration and ordered me to put the gun up because it wasn't worth it. I stood in the middle of the floor flooded with tears. Mike was still trying to apologize as Mary my neighbor came over to console me. The people I love the most always end up hurting me.

I was trembling and then suddenly spazzed out of control, throwing every item that Mike owned out onto the lawn, which wasn't much.

"Bitch, what the hell are you doing?" he yelled.

"What I should have done a long time ago, you dirty bastard!"

The officer told Mike to watch his language and to vacate the premises immediately.

The officer, Officer McCoy, returned with a pep talk, gave me his card, and told me to call anytime. He couldn't understand men like Mike who have a good woman and find a way to screw it up.

After everyone left, I cleaned up the mess that I made and called a security company over to change the locks. I needed to feel safe and when that's complete, I'm filing for a divorce.

My life just became a Lifetime movie. First the shit with Camille now, Mike's betrayal. How much can a woman take? I see why Camille is going crazy. I cried off and on, then I finally gathered myself together and checked the missed calls I had on my phone.

I just knew they were from Mike so I didn't bother. "This is bullshit!" I yelled.

I was so angry at the fact that Mike brought Jose to my home thinking I was out of town. I knew about the affair, just the overall disrespect.

I needed time to think, I was losing it. I needed to take a leave of absence from work to get my life back in order. I started first with calling my job, then I called a relative of mine to watch the house and gather my mail. My cousin, Vanessa, was a person I trusted, so she didn't mind, as well as Mary, my neighbor. She has a key and I have a key to her house whenever she is away. It helps to keep people from breaking in.

I thought about heading back to Atlanta for Camille's sake. My mind has been on that baby since I left.

I called Mary over and talked to her about my upcoming plan and confided in her what was going on and the incident with Camille. Mary's first instinct was to turn Camille in and if I didn't, she would. I told Mary to keep her mouth shut! If I can't get through to her, then she leaves me with no choice.

"That baby needs to be home with his mother and I have to talk sense into her," I said to Mary.

She was in total shock with what I confessed to her. She promised she wouldn't say anything until I reported back, but was going to pray in the process.

After Mary left I started packing again, and then found myself sitting in a daze. I knew meeting Jose would lead me to Mike's infidelities, but gay was never on my list. I listened to all of Mike's voice messages and cried. The thought of being alone scares me, but my overall health scares me more. The man that I love was putting my health at risk. Just the thought of him raw doggin' me and Jose didn't sit well with me. I was desperate, but not that damn desperate.

Chapter 22

Camille

I'd called Nikki several times and still no answer. If she knew like I knew, she had better not be avoiding me. That's the last thing she should do!

I reached for my baby and scanned the channel back to the news. Michelle and Greg were on…again…giving another news conference pleading with the kidnappers. I sat back and laughed at those clowns.

I couldn't help but notice how good Michelle looked for someone who had multiple stab wounds. "I should have killed you!" I said to the TV screen.

Greg released a picture of the baby referencing a birthmark on his chin, something I never noticed until now and there it was plain as day.

"Well little one, I guess we'll be hibernating for a bit," I said, as I played with him. The baby started whining and I knew it was his feeding time. I tried to breast feed him but he got louder and louder. I'd always wanted to breast feed – the baby is so much attached to its mother that way.

The baby kept crying and I got frustrated. "Damn it, what's wrong?" The television was getting on my nerves, the baby cried, I hadn't heard anything from Greg, and Nikki wouldn't pick up.

I slammed the remote against the end table and instantly, the baby got quiet. I tried feeding him again but he wouldn't latch on to my nipple. He screamed louder.

"Your whining ass is getting a bottle," I hollered. All this noise was uncalled for. I went to the kitchen and heated a bottle in the microwave. When I stuck it in the baby's mouth, he screamed like crazy, and milk foamed out of his mouth. The milk squirted out of the bottle.

"Shit, this milk is hot! Oh, my baby, I'm so sorry!" I ran to the kitchen and got a bottle at room temperature. I tried to give it to him, cradling and comforting him. He finally took the bottle, but still sniffed as he drank. "Mommy is so sorry," I whispered, as I cuddled him in my arms.

My mind was so off. I waited to hear from Greg but there was no action on my end of the phone. As a matter of fact, there has not been action in the last few days from my phone. I hoped he didn't locate the chip. I was pissed off because he made this relationship very difficult for me.

Finally the baby was down, but still sniffed as he fell asleep. I felt so bad for not checking the bottle.

My phone finally rang and it was Nikki's ass. "So, are you dodging my calls now?" I said, when I answered.

"No, I had shit going on!" she shot back. I spoke with her briefly. She updated me on the situation with Mike and his gay lover Jose. Nikki said she's coming back as soon as she handles her business in a day or two to get away.

I begged Nikki to stay home; I didn't need her anymore. She yelled she was coming and hung up!

Damn, she's coming back to screw things up I bet. I heard helicopters and peeped out the window. Didn't see anything but noticed a parked car slightly across the street and thought that was strange because I never saw it there before. Maybe someone's car stopped, I thought. Just then, Greg's Mercedes pulled up in my driveway. I almost fell trying to get to the baby. I quickly picked him up and headed upstairs. Thank God he was already asleep.

I heard the doorbell ring before I could get the baby in his room and turn on his light. The baby squirmed and I prayed he didn't wake up; I had to hurry and make my way back down stairs. Finally, I tucked in all visible baby items and went to unlock the door with a sweat.

"What took you so long?" Greg asked when I opened the door.

"I was in a deep sleep," I said as I yawned. "What's up? What are you doing here?"

"That's all I get is a what's up?" Greg shot back.

"I'm not sure what you mean, but do come in."

As bad as I wanted to jump his bones, I played along to whatever mood he was in. Besides I wanted to see what his visit was about this time.

"What brings you by?" I asked. "I haven't heard from you, nor have you answered any of my calls."

His answer surprised me. "You...that's what brings me by," he said, politely, before leaning in to kiss me.

I thought about the micro-chip, but instead I kissed him back hard. I wanted him so badly I started to unzip his pants and knelt down in front of him.

"Camille, no! Not now."

"When then Greg, what's wrong with now?" I asked, looking confused.

He backed up and told me how tired and stressed he was, that he was not in the mood for lovemaking but admitted he did miss me. He also said he couldn't accept my calls because he was at the hospital and dealing with the detectives, so that made it impossible to talk.

I expressed how badly I missed him and that I needed him as well. I continued to fondle him and, finally, he gave in. I unbuttoned his shirt and sucked on his nipples. He stopped me and asked me to pour him a drink. I stopped what I was doing and ran to the kitchen to open a bottle of Pinot Grigio. I poured two glasses and made my way back to him. Anything Greg asked for I did with no hesitation. I sat the glasses down on my glass coffee table and went back into the kitchen to get coasters. He was all smiles when I returned and made a toast to "us."

"To us!" I repeated. I couldn't wait any longer. I gulped down my wine then quickly made my way to his erection and straddled him; I pleasured him with my mouth as he moaned.

"Baby, I'm glad you found your way back to us. Maybe we can be a family when it's all over with," I said, as I massaged his balls.

"What do you mean *us*, Camille? And what family?" Greg said raising his voice.

I laughed, trying to play it off. He tried to sit up and I pushed him back on the couch, "Babe, relax. 'To us!' Remember?"

I got on top of him and glided up and down. Greg moaned as if he was into it but I knew better. It was like he was pretending and I noticed everything. He gripped my ass and slapped it a couple times but was very aggressive, these were hard slaps. He became deranged as he started pulling my hair, then flipping me over the couch. I fell to the floor. He got on top of me and pinned me down once I hit the floor. I couldn't move. I struggled with him and I tried to get up.

"Greg! What the hell is wrong with you? Stop it!" I said, trying to get up.

He looked at me with blood shot eyes, huffing and puffing as he fought to keep me pinned to the floor. I continued to struggle, but I was unable to get through to him until I kicked him in the groin.

"Greg, what is going on?" I demanded an answer.

He jumped up, limping as he grabbed his balls, and started to get dressed without saying a single word. I felt light-headed and dizzy. The room started spinning. My body got hot and sweat came over me. The last thing I remembered, before I passed out, was Greg standing over me with a wicked look on his face.

Chapter 23

Greg

"Camille...Camille...wake up!" I said, calling her name out. I tried shaking the bitch, still no response.

I couldn't take much more of this charade any longer. I slipped some Rohypnol in her glass of wine after she made a second trip back to the kitchen for those coasters. It would only leave her unconscious for a while. I'm glad she didn't detect anything; it was tasteless and odorless, and she wouldn't have a clue.

I cleaned myself, slipped her clothes back on, carried her upstairs, and dumped her ass on the bed like trash.

I searched through her house looking for anything suspicious. I checked her closets, drawers, cushions, clothes, attic, and looked under her bed, nothing! "Shit, I know she has something here," I said. I went through and checked the closets again; this time I detected an odor but I couldn't find out where it was coming from.

"Purse, where is her purse?" I started panicking.

I ran downstairs looking for her purse, phone, and checked her fridge, which was pretty much empty. I glanced in her laundry room and noticed a bottle of *Dreft* laundry detergent, the one that's used for babies.

I checked the washer and dryer, nothing was in them. I finally went into the dining room and found her purse, emptied it out. I found nothing, but came across a key. . I found two cell phones – one was disposable– and my thoughts were all over the place. I called my number from the disposable phone to lock the number in and deleted the call from her phone log. I went through and jotted down a number that had just called minutes before I got there. I wasn't sure what good it would do, but maybe it will help.

"Think, think, think Greg!" I was going crazy.

There was a foul odor coming from somewhere that I couldn't detect. I ran upstairs to check her closet again and came across a pacifier holder. I mumbled "What the hell is she doing with this?" I looked out into the room where she was still passed out and checked behind her pillows. Lo and behold I found a baby onesie. "But where was the baby, a monitor or something?" I wondered.

I freaked out. I got up, walked over to Camille laid out on the bed, and spat on her, "Bitch, I should kill your psychotic ass," I said as I walked off. I put the pacifier holder in a zip lock bag, stuck the onesie in my coat, and looked around again before I exited the door.

Before I could turn the key in the ignition, I saw a note under my windshield wiper. I opened the door to get the note as I noticed the detectives out of the corner of my eye approaching me.

"Detectives, what are you doing here?" I asked in shock.

"Question is…what are *you* doing here, Greg?" Detective Floyd asked.

"Visiting a friend."

"Would that be your mistress, Camille Young?" he asked, with a smirk on his face.

"Greg, we need you to come down to the precinct for questioning," Detective Ball said.

Fuck! I closed the car door, and noticed the detectives leaving. These bastards have been following my every move. I was at my ex-mistress' house while my wife was recovering in the hospital was definitely not a good look. This will be a media frenzy. "Greg, this doesn't look good," I kept telling myself while driving. I couldn't believe this shit. Here I was, an hour away from picking up Michelle to take her home, and now I have to go to the precinct. Hopefully it won't take long, since they have nothing on me.

I had no choice but to come clean with Michelle about Camille. Never in a million years, did I think that I would end up in a situation like this. The media will have a field day with this information.

I dialed both Michelle and Dianne but got no answer. I dialed Michelle back and left a message telling her that I would be late picking her up from the hospital, and then hung up.

Out of all days, this had to be the worst one!

Chapter 24

Greg

It had been over forty-five minutes that I had been down at the precinct for questioning. I couldn't believe that those bastards though I had something to do with my son's disappearance. I yelled at one detective who clearly said I tried to have my wife killed. I finally revealed the real reason why I was visiting Camille's place and told them about the baby items I recovered, that way they could focus on Camille's involvement instead.

Detective Ball laughed so hard that I was getting real irritated with the bastard. "Now you're planting items to cover your track, is that it?" One of the other interrogators in the room laughed as well like this was a joking matter.

"You fat bastard!" I said.

"That's it, get it all out Greg," Detective Ball responds.

I got so fed up that I told them what they needed to know and they didn't believe a word I said. Now I have been interrogated for over two hours now. I put my hand over my face and shook my head, "Can this get any worse?" I thought.

I almost lost my cool from all the questions they were asking. "When did the affair start? Could she have done this? Did I help her? What's Camille's motive? Did you leave Michelle at home that day alone on purpose?" Then everything began to sound like blah, blah, blah...

The questions kept coming. I knew these questions were basic protocol because of me being an attorney. Now I'd found myself in a situation when I was the one used to representing clients in the same ones.

After two and a half hours, I was finally able to leave the station, but not without a dozen reporters standing outside. As I made my way past them, I checked my phone and was shocked to find that I had 26 missed calls, and several voicemail messages.

I tried to get to the hospital as fast as I could, but knew I was in big trouble. I thought about calling Michelle to see if she'd left, but was afraid of what she might say. For some reason, I got a feeling that a piece of information would make it on the evening news, since they had been reporting about the case on a regular basis. I really just wanted to take Michelle home and talk to her alone.

When I got to the hospital, I wasn't surprised to find more reporters, but I fought my way through and made it to the 4th floor. The moment I exited the elevator, I was met with glares from both Michelle and Dianne.

"Baby, I'm so sorry I'm late, you won't believe what happened," I said, trying to smooth over the situation.

"Greg, save it!" she snapped. The look on her face spoke volumes.

"Greg, I got your message," Dianne said. "But we didn't know you would be this late. Michelle has been waiting for hours and she wanted you to take her home."

"Again, I'm sorry, but I'm here now," I said, moving to take control of the wheelchair. The car is parked out front.

"Greg, don't bother," Michelle interrupted. "When you get home, I want you to pack your shit and get out of the house!"

"What?" I said, sounding confused. The elevator was still opened and people were staring.

"You heard me; as a matter of fact take your shit to that bitch, Camille's house!" she spat, as Dianne wheeled her onto the elevator.

I hopped in the elevator just as it was about to close and for once I was speechless. I was so embarrassed, that I couldn't face the truth of Michelle's word that spat at me. I didn't even take notice of Michelle's red eyes.

"I guess you're speechless now!" Michelle said turning her attention to Dianne.

"Michelle, can we talk?" I asked, desperately.

"Dianne, please take me home," Michelle said, ignoring me. Dianne did as she was told, and left me dumbfounded. I watched as Michelle pulled off with Dianne.

On the way to my car, I ran into a concerned Ed who had come to the hospital thinking something had happened since I never returned his calls or text.

"Man, I've been trying to reach you all day. We need to talk about what I found out!" Ed said.

"Found out about what? What's going on Ed?"

"Camille's background record and physician report."

Ed revealed that Camille was once married before when her husband was killed in a freak accident. Her husband Walter was leaving her for another woman, whom he fathered a child with, and wanted out of the marriage with Camille. They just so happened to be out for dinner together to discuss the divorce agreement. On the way home, a truck driver struck their car when Walter swerved into the wrong lane. She suffered some major injuries, but he died. Some of the people Ed interviewed think he was poisoned, but it was never confirmed because an autopsy was never performed.

"So what does this have to do with me?" I asked him.

"You're doing the exact same thing Walter did to her, in her eyes, and someone like her will easily flip the script, Greg."

Ed also added that Camille had a hysterectomy, so she's unable to have kids, a reason why she focused only on the baby rather than Michelle during the attack.

"I need to get back over there, Ed. I need to tear that house apart because something is missing. I need answers! I had to go down to the precinct and answer questions, now Michelle is pissed. She knows about Camille, man." The palm of my hands started to sweat. "Ed, the detectives think I had my baby kidnapped, on top of that you tell me this shit about Camille's past."

"Well, don't say anything to anyone; I'm going to represent you if it comes to that."

"It might just come to that. When I was at her house, there were some questionable baby items that I took. I just know she's behind this mess."

"This situation has gotten way out of control; we need to act now to bring your son back safe!"

"Man, Ed I'm going crazy! I don't know what to do! Michelle wants nothing to do with me, this broad has baby shit in her house that I'm sure belongs to my baby but I can't prove it! I don't even give a fuck about business right now, I just want my wife and baby and my life back to how it should be!"

"We have to act fast! Just stay focused on bringing your son home, I don't need you to flip out now."

"Man, I really have to get home and talk to Michelle. I don't know what's going on anymore; it's beyond my control now. She is really trying to screw me, man. What did I get myself into?"

I felt like we needed to go to the police with the information Ed provided, but knew we really didn't have enough information to have her arrested just yet. Ed said he was filing a motion to have Walter's body exhumed for an autopsy and more testing, so that they can have enough evidence to present to the District Attorney.

"Thanks, man, I really appreciate it. I don't know what I'd do without you," I said, giving him a bear hug. "Let me head home to my wife so that I can explain to her what's really going on and the actual truth," I said.

I noticed spectators whispering as I backed my car out and sped from the parking lot as I looked back in my rear view mirror.

* * *

I pulled in the garage and felt anxiety wash over me. I prayed one more time before entering the house because I didn't know what to expect.

I spoke to Dianne who was very dry; I understand she's Michelle's close friend, but this clearly did not have anything to do with her. I continued upstairs to the bedroom and noticed Michelle was sleeping. I wanted to wake her, but decided not to. I sat in the recliner staring at her hoping she would wake so that we could talk.

Thirty minutes passed when Michelle finally woke up from what seemed like a bad dream, she tossed and cried out of her sleep. She must have feared the worst when she mumbled, "Jr., Jr." I ran to her side to calm her. She opened her eyes, jumped, then lashed out at me as she pushed me away. I pleaded for us to talk so that I could explain everything to her.

Michelle screamed for me to get out, that she couldn't deal with me right now.

I looked at Michelle through her tears from the pain I had caused her. I wanted to stay, but I knew she needed some space. I walked out of the room, grabbed my keys, and headed back to the garage, banging my head on the steering wheel once inside the car.

"Dammit, what have I done? This can't be happening to me," I said, beating the steering wheel. I wanted to cry so badly but my mind started to spin. As I sat there a thought came to mind and I needed to do something drastic for the sake of my family.

Chapter 25

Michelle

I couldn't understand why I was going through what seemed to be one nightmare after the other. I pleaded with God to help me understand why this was happening. I lived right, and didn't bother anyone. But I felt like I was being attacked at every angle. My son was taken right in front of my eyes, which made me more depressed than ever. And now Greg betrayed me, something I would never expect from him. His betrayal threw me for a loop. Never in a million years would I have thought my marriage was in jeopardy.

Every time I go to sleep, I have nightmares of that tragic day. I prayed to God that whoever took my baby was treating him well. Deep down in my heart I knew he was still alive. I kept seeing this image of that woman behind her mask of makeup and wig.

Dianne came upstairs and read me a couple of scriptures to help keep me faithful and sane. The phone rang off the hook. I knew it was my mom, and probably a slew of relatives wanting information that I didn't have to give. We turned on the news to hear the latest and CNN started reporting the kidnapping as a set up to cover Greg's affair with a clear picture of the woman Camille Young.

"Oh, my God!" Dianne shouted. I was in total shock when they reported that just hours before that, Greg was seen leaving her home. There were photographs all over the screen to back it up.

"How stupid can he be?" I muttered. "That bastard!" I yelled in pain. "How could he do this? They reported him being at her house for over an hour while I waited for him at the hospital." Dianne cradle me like a newborn, I was so lost for words that I became numb.

"Camille, Camille, that's her! I screamed. "Oh, no Dianne, it can't be," I said emerging from her arm.

"What is it, Michelle?"

"It's her; I know it is, the pictures from Troy…Dianne, she resembles every bit of the kidnapper behind the wig and makeup I know it's her, the mole!" I screamed, in panic.

"Michelle, please calm down. We're not sure nor do we have any proof."

I told Dianne my scars are proof enough! I ran and emptied the contents out my purse searching for the card I found with her initials. "Dianne you see this?" I held up the card and the very line I recalled and said aloud was *"I wished it was me instead of you. Keep your family close."* as I shoved the card in Dianne's face. "She wished she had Greg's baby instead. You see, Dianne, I'm not crazy."

"Michelle, I don't know, but you do have a point. It's strange she showed up at the hospital that day. Was she planning on taking the baby then, I wonder? Dianne said as she contemplated.

"Exactly!" I told Dianne it was time to meet this Camille chick, she obviously knew me but I didn't have a clue about her. She has something that belongs to me! First my husband, then my son – nobody messes with my family.

"Dianne, please help me get my baby back!" I begged.

"Michelle, I have your back. I trust your instincts."

I thanked Dianne for helping me. I then walk over to my closet and pulled down a black box, unlocked it, and took out my .38 Special.

"Michelle, what are you doing?" Dianne said in fear.

"Protecting me and mine, I will not be a victim in my own home again! We both jumped once we heard the doorbell and it always takes me back to that fateful day. I looked out the window and saw the detectives from the hospital. I also saw them on the security monitor Greg had installed standing near the front door.

I put the gun away and Dianne and I both headed downstairs. I opened the door and greeted the men as they followed me into the den.

The short round detective, Ball, stated they dropped by to inform us that baby items were found not far from where the van was ditched. It is simply procedure for them to reach out to families when someone was missing in case the items belonged to that missing person. He went on to explain that it may not be my child's items, but they will be checked for prints and stains.

I was in tears, but had hoped that my baby was safe somewhere out there.

"Mrs. Langston," Detective Floyd said.

"Call me Michelle," I responded.

"With the new information that has surfaced regarding your husband's mistress, can you tell us anything else?" He asked.

I looked at the detective in disbelief. I was already upset, now he asked about my husband's mistress? "Detective, I don't know anything. I just found out actually, but after looking at the woman's picture, she really resembles the attacker," I said.

I also explained about the day I gave birth and a woman came to the hospital with a gift basket. Something happened and it was left at the front desk. Dianne went to grab the card and brought it back downstairs to give to the detectives.

They read the card, looked at the initials, then looked at each other. "This means nothing. Did you write this Michelle?"

"Detectives, that's enough," Dianne said. "It's time for you all to go now."

Just as they were headed out, Greg walks in.

"Detectives, what are you all doing here?" Greg asks.

Detective Floyd smirked as Greg walked by. He looked back and said, "We'll be in touch," and left.

"This is a big mess," I thought.

"Greg, this is all your fault!" I yelled. I was so angry that I started to hyperventilate. Greg grabbed me and held me tight; I cried in his arms.

Chapter 26

Nikki

After the incident with Mike, I contemplated going back to Atlanta to Camille's, but needed some time away and to check on that baby, who was constantly on my mind.

I was able to talk to a divorce attorney and speak with Officer McCoy on several occasions after he felt the need to check on me.

I was granted some time off from my job to deal with my personal issues and evaluate my life. I have enough money saved to get me by. I just needed to take some time for me.

Mike called me everyday begging for me to speak with him and had the audacity to send me roses. Where he got the money from I didn't know. At one point I considered taking him back to keep from ending up like Camille, but the thought of him putting my life in danger was a risk I wasn't willing to revisit. He has walked over me long enough.

I really needed someone to talk to because Camille wasn't stable. She used to be the one I would call when I needed to talk, but she can't help me, she has issues of her own.

My thoughts were interrupted when Officer McCoy decided to stop by. We engaged in small talk. I didn't know what it was that Officer McCoy found so interesting about me, but he began coming around often. When I found out how much we had in common, I actually became more and more comfortable. I had no problem letting him know the amount of stress I had been under and even told him of my plans to visit Atlanta, which he was in favor of.

He said he could drive down on the weekend and hang out if I wanted. I considered his invite since I had nothing to lose.

I walked him to the door just in time for Mike to see me give him a hug, and then he sped off in his truck. McCoy just laughed, I said goodbye and went back inside.

Chapter 27

Nikki

The drive to Atlanta wasn't bad, just tiring. I should have driven the first time instead of taking the bus. I ate a slew of junk food while riding down 229. I felt good for some reason. It was sunny and cool, but still a beautiful day; I just hoped it doesn't turn out to be gloomy once I get to Camille's house.

I jammed all the way through rush hour traffic. Toni Braxton blasted through the speakers, "He wasn't man enough for me..." "Sing it girl! He wasn't shit!" I added, while I laughed and fought back tears. My phone rang. I looked at the number and it was Mike again. I decided to answer for the hell of it.

"Yes, Mike."

"Babe, can we talk?"

"Mike, what is it?"

"I just want to apologize. I wanted to stop by, but when I saw you with that lunatic officer, I kept going. Why were you hugging on him?" he asked, trying to sound jealous.

"Mike, you're not sorry. You're sorry you got caught with your gay ass. And who I hug is not your concern anymore. I hope you have a great life!" I said and hung up. The nerve of his ass worrying about who I'm hugging, how dare he!

He called repeatedly for 10 minutes straight. I ignored all calls.

My phone rang again and I decided to answer, this time I wasn't going to play nice. I answered without looking at the Caller ID. "What the hell do you want this time?"

"Huh! I'm sorry, Nikki? This is David…Officer McCoy."

"Oh, David, I'm so sorry. I thought you were Mike calling again like he's crazy," I responded.

"I guess he's trying to win you back," he chuckled. "Did you make it to your destination?" he asked.

"Actually, I am pulling up now as we speak."

"Please call me back once you get settled, if you would love to talk more."

"David what do you see in me that interests you, I'm no skinny Minnie or beauty queen."

"Nikki you are definitely a queen, let no one tell you any different. We have a lot in common and I enjoy the conversations we share. You are a beautiful woman regardless of your size."

I smiled but was really lost for words. I ended the call with a promise to call him back.

I got out of the car, grabbed my luggage, and rang the doorbell.

"Nikki, what are you doing back here?" Camille asked while looking around paranoid.

"I told you I was coming back," I said, as I walked in past her.

I asked Camille if something was bothering her; she said no, but seemed shaken up. I wasn't so sure. I watched her because she was acting strange.

"Where is the baby?" I said out of concern.

"Upstairs, I'm going to get him now."

When she came back down with the baby, I saw that his mouth was blistered.

"Camille, what happened to him?" I said, as I walked towards them.

"Nothing to worry about. Just a burn from the milk, it was too hot."

Oh my, I desperately had to get this baby away from her; Camille was delusional and twisted. She didn't know how to care for a baby, better yet herself.

Camille finally warmed up to the fact that I was there and not leaving anytime soon. She opened up about Greg's recent visit and why she couldn't remember anything. When she woke up, she had a terrible bruise on her leg and couldn't figure out how it got there. Camille still felt light headed and the room seemed to be spinning. She couldn't remember much, but she did remember Greg being there. Camille must have fallen asleep, but the aches and pains she was experiencing seemed out of the blue.

"Nikki, I just hope Greg didn't do anything that he will regret later on."

"Where was the baby while you were out of it, Camille?"

"In the closet screaming. When I went in to check on him, he had shit all out his diaper. I'm so glad that room is sound proof."

I took the baby from her as she walked around arguing with someone who wasn't in the house. That alarmed me. I prayed to God that whatever was going on with her, I had to keep this baby near. There is no telling what she was capable of doing.

Chapter 28

Camille

I dialed Greg's number several times but no answer, "Mother fuck!" I realized the light on my phone hasn't flashed in a very long time and I think he figured out his phone was tapped.

"Camille," Nikki called out.

"Not now, Nikki!" I said. "Damn, what is she really doing here?" I mumbled, "She has to go."

I needed to find Greg, but was not going to let the baby out my sight. I knew he was up to something. Then it dawned on me, the wine bottle I saw on the counter, I remember it being on my shelf. I went downstairs to see if I could recall anything. All of my wine glasses were put away, but couldn't remember drinking any wine.

I think it's time to let Greg know who was in charge! I programmed Greg's home number in my phone while he was sleeping; I figured I would call until he picked up. I picked up the phone and dialed.

"Hello," the woman on the other end answered in a rhapsody voice.

"May I speak with Greg? It's Camille…"

"Camille who?" the woman asked.

"Camille Young."

"Bitch don't call my house again, you really have some nerve. What's your damn problem?" she said. Then I heard Greg pick up, "Camille?"

"Yes, babe, you didn't pick up on your cell, so I figured I would try you here," I said, nonchalantly.

"Don't you ever call here again or disrespect my wife or home. You got that? What the hell is wrong with you, Camille? You are really delusional!" Greg said and hung up.

"So it's like that," I said, yelling through the phone like he could hear me. I started throwing things around and cutting up the sheets. "I bet he won't disrespect me again, after it's all said and done!"

"Camille, is everything okay in here?" Nikki asked, peeking in the room.

"Yes! Damn it…Ugh."

I tried to calm down and catch my breath when the doorbell startled me. Nikki brought the baby up. I looked out the window and didn't see anyone, so I went to ask who was at the door. It was the postman with a package. I didn't order nor was I expecting anything. I looked around before I signed for the package, then stepped outside the door to see if anyone was near. Finally I walked back inside and locked the door behind me.

"Nikki came back downstairs, playing with the baby.

I opened the package. It was filled with photos of the getaway van, a lady that looked like me, pictures of Greg and me together, and a punctured voodoo doll. "What the hell?" I looked at the lady in the picture and you clearly couldn't see her face. I ran to the door with the pictures in tow and I saw no one. I walked back inside the house to regroup.

"Camille, what is that?"

"Here, take a look for yourself."

I paced the floor, tracing back my every move. "This can't be, he's not trying to play me with these mind games, someone will get hurt, I promise you," I said, pacing the floor.

"Camille, let Greg go; we will find you someone else who appreciates you. This is getting ugly and someone's been watching your every move."

"Nikki, shut up! Damn, you've been rambling since you got here, just because your shit didn't work out don't mean mine won't," I snapped at her.

"Camille, go to hell! I've been nothing but good to you. You are spinning out of control. If I leave, I will take the baby," Nikki said.

"You won't be taking a baby out of my house, you ain't that bold Nikki! Just try it!" I said, daring her to do it.

Nikki cut her eyes at me, as if she wanted to say something. "If I go down, you go down, you hear me?"

"Yes, Camille. Loud and clear!"

I grabbed the package, my baby, and headed back upstairs, leaving Nikki where she belonged, by herself. I checked my cell phone and had several missed calls from an unknown number. Someone has to be playing games, but they better come with something more than these pictures.

The phone rang again so I answered.

"You got your package I see; it's just a matter of time before I take you out," the voice on the other end said.

"Very clever hiding behind photos, Michelle, don't you think this is an awkward way to meet? No wonder Greg is leaving your silly ass!" I said, laughing like hell through the phone.

"You hurt that baby and I swear you won't breathe again! Got that!" CLICK

The nerve of that bitch! I have something she wants and will never get back. I think we'll meet soon, this time I will make sure she's out of the picture for good.

Chapter 29

Greg

Michelle blamed me for the entire situation. I held her in my arms tight for as long as she let me.

When she proceeded up the stairway the phone rang; it was Detective Ball informing us that the baby items found were not Greg Jr.'s. I immediately fell to my knees and thanked God; it gave me hope.

I started up the stairs when I heard the phone ring again, this time Michelle answered, and I heard her say, "Camille?"

I ran downstairs and grabbed the phone in the kitchen. I couldn't believe she was calling my house. I cursed her out badly and then hung up.

I went to Michelle, informed her of Detective Ball's call, and talked to her about Camille. This time Michelle agreed to listen, as I spilled my guts about a woman I had relations with and why I thought she was behind the kidnapping. My tears started flowing and it was all guilt. I apologized to Michelle for hurting her and the pain I put her through.

She looked at me and asked, "Why? Why her?" I simply didn't have an answer for her.

I told Michelle I stopped seeing Camille and that's when everything started happening. I admitted to her it was Camille outside the hospital room that day with the gift basket, which Michelle already knew, and how Camille knew we were there by tapping my phone with a micro-chip.

Michelle stated we would deal with our situation after we find our son and that she needed to know just what Camille was capable of so she knew what kind of person she were dealing with.

I told Michelle that Ed would be over shortly to go over something he came across regarding Camille's background. I didn't think Camille would harm our son because she wanted a life with me, I told Michelle. I could see in her eyes that it made her sick every time I mentioned Camille's name.

I didn't know what Michelle was thinking, but I wished she would say something. I walked over to her and held her in my arms; she held me back with no problem.

An hour passed, it was getting dark and I was mentally drained. Michelle and Dianne left the house soon after Ed arrived.

He had a file folder containing several documents.

"Are these the documents from earlier?"

"Yes, sir."

Ed explained that the judge signed an order to search Camille's home. He also stated that Walter's body has been exhumed and the lab results should be ready soon. From talking to Camille's therapist, Ed shared that Camille is troubled and has a bipolar disorder disconnecting her from reality. She seems normal for a while, but when things don't go her way, it's hell to pay.

Ed had Camille's therapy session documents; the dates went way back into the 90's, and her family history. She disconnected herself from her family and hadn't spoken to them in ages including a brother that I didn't know existed. I couldn't believe all that I was hearing and reading – this girl had multiple personalities.

I told Ed I called the number I found in Camille's second phone and it belonged to a Nikki Martin per her voicemail. Ed said he would look into it. Perhaps she could have been the getaway driver during the kidnapping. It dawned on me that this could be her accomplice.

Ed came up with another dumb plan to get Camille alone again, which was not going to work but whatever plan we come up with, we needed Michelle on board and that won't be easy.

If only I had stayed away and kept my pants up, I would not be in this predicament today.

Chapter 30

Michelle

I parked a block from Camille's house and we walked to keep from being seen by anyone. I looked at the address I had written down and noticed the police squad leaving her home with a bag. Dianne and I hid behind a tree and watched as they talked, then finally they got into their cars and drove off. After waiting for five minutes, we went around back and came across her back patio. I tip toed up the steps with Dianne who was behind me.

Dianne leaned in against the siding so she would not be seen. I saw a light come on in a room up top, and I decided to climb up. I stood on the wood rail trying to keep my balance. I pulled out my phone, and called Camille's number several times, hanging up each time. I heard her in a room not far from where I was leaning in, cursing and screaming. Then I heard another female's voice and that's when Dianne and I looked at each other.

I tried my best to get as close to the window as possible, but my body was aching from the climbing and I felt my leg giving out. I called her number again and hung up.

"Call here again," I heard her say.

"Camille, what is it?" the other lady asked.

"Someone keeps calling here playing on my phone. I know it's her," she said.

"Camille, keep calm or you will blow your cover," the other lady said.

"Cover," I whispered when Dianne told me to hush. "Did you hear that Dianne?"

"Yes!"

"Nikki, you're right. That bitch is just mad because Greg is leaving her and she will be left with nothing…no son or a husband and I will get both," she said, laughing.

"BITCH," I said in anger, as I slid off the wood rail and fell on my ass.

"Who's there," we heard someone say.

Dianne helped me up and we managed to run before lights from all angles came on. We made it to the car just as I started limping because I hit my foot on a stump. My leg ached from the accident.

"Michelle, hurry. Let's get to the house," Dianne said in fear.

"Dianne, she has my son!"

"Michelle, I know. After the lady said something about blowing her cover I turned on the recorder on my phone to catch the rest of the conversation."

"Oh my God, you are a genius!" I said thanking her, but I was in a lot of pain.

I couldn't help but think of my son. I looked at the pictures I took on my phone every day of him asleep in his sleeper the day he was taken. We received daily updates on the search effort and still there was nothing. I heard Camille's remarks over and over in my head, which made me wonder where she has my son hidden since she's still there. Obviously, the police didn't find anything.

Dianne promised to stay until we got the baby back.

Once home, I limped upstairs to soak my foot, but found Greg in the recliner waiting.

"Baby, what happened?"

"I fell, stumped my foot, and sprained my ankle at Camille's."

"At Camille's? Baby, what the hell were you doing there?" he asked raising an eye brow.

"Looking for my son!" I said, while in tears hearing Camille's statement in my head. Greg asked what happened.

I called Dianne into the room, we explained why we went there and what we overheard standing out back near her window. Dianne played the recording from her phone

Once Greg heard the recording, he knew he had to take action fast. He filled me and Dianne in on Ed's findings from Camille's background check, Walters's death, and her mental disorder.

We all brain stormed, but came up with nothing. Getting her alone didn't mean the baby would surface; I just knew I would end up dealing with her on my own, dead or alive.

Dianne left the room and I asked Greg, "How did you get involved with a lunatic? Why would you risk our family for a piece of ass?"

His reply was the same as the first, "It just happened, I don't know." Me falling off a bike just happened, but stumbling on a dick is my choice. I continued to play it cool with him until this whole ordeal was over.

Camille wasn't that crazy, she clearly knows what she's doing. Using that as an excuse wasn't going to fly with me, she wasn't crazy, I'll show her crazy.

Greg's eyes followed me as I stood up. When I pulled the gun out from behind my back, he went ballistic.

"Michelle, what are you planning on doing with that?" Greg asked.

"What I should have done weeks ago when that bitch stepped foot into my home!"

Chapter 31

Michelle

My head was throbbing when I woke up. My leg hurt, my body was sore, but I still kept moving despite the pain I was in. I headed downstairs to the smell of breakfast. I grabbed some aspirin out the cabinet and chased it down with orange juice.

Greg had cooked a buffet, I wasn't sure for whom. I opened the morning paper and sat at the table. On the front page was Greg and Camille, the headline read: *"Victim and His Mistress, Could It Be This Was All an Act of Jealousy."*

There were two pictures splashed on the front page. The first was of Greg when he arrived at Camille's house, and the second was of a kiss that was captured by someone watching them closely from inside her home. I sank in my chair and felt sick as I read the article.

Greg brought me a plate and I politely pushed it away. I jammed the paper in his hands.

"Damn, what is it now?"

He looks at the paper, read the article, and responds, "Baby, this is not what it looks like. I can explain."

Although he told me why he went there that day, I didn't know about the kiss, but what does it matter anyway. He already admitted to cheating with that whore, and I was not interested in hearing more lies.

"Greg, just save it. I can't stomach anymore of this mess, I'm not in the mood."

My mom called non-stop and left voicemails. My dad wanted to kill Greg so badly.

This situation drained me. My weight fluctuated, my hair fell out due to stress, and my health wasn't the best. I lived a simple life. I never thought about killing anyone until now; it had all taken a toll on me.

Dianne came downstairs saying Nancy Grace was having a ball with this story; she had to turn off the television.

I told Greg to take care of his mistress or I would.

"What do you mean take care of her Michelle?"

"Just what it sounded like." I was so sick of it all that I was about to take matters into my own hands.

I didn't know Greg like I thought I did or else I would have figured him out. We still had people out there searching for our son, but they continued to come up empty-handed. I felt the urge to help look, but I found myself kneeling before God praying with all I had left.

"God, please send me a sign, I know I am a good person, but lately things have been happening to me that I just can't figure out and need some understanding. Please, for my sake, let my son be okay and to bring him home soon. Wherever he is, Lord, I pray for his safety and protection. In Jesus' name, Amen!"

Standing, I felt weak; I needed some strength to deal with my situation head on. I needed to call my mom who was worried to death. She flew back to Texas right after the baby was born, then came back to help with the search, and then flew back home. Now she wished she would have stayed with all that has happened. I got my nerve up to call her with my dad on the other end and cried like a baby. They were concerned and asked questions about all that's been on the news. I answered some and was vague with the other questions. I promised I wouldn't make any drastic decisions until this was over and my son was found safe. I told her to stay put. No need to fly here, I would be okay, but Greg, on the other hand, was not safe with my dad.

I looked up and saw Greg standing in the door way as I ended the call with my parents. Greg followed me as I went to wash my face. He stated how concerned he was about my state of mind and health. I finally made my way back to the bedroom as I sat and ate the plate of food he brought up. I was within inches of stepping over the line when it came to the idea of killing Camille.

"Greg, you know this lady has ruined our lives."

"Yes, I'm totally responsible Michelle and apologize for my actions. I wish I could take it all back."

"No need, I've heard your apologies too many times. Too bad you didn't do a background check first before bedding her or else…"

Greg looked at me in tears and said he never meant for this to happen or to hurt anyone. That I believed. He cried, sniffed, cried, sniffed, but it still wasn't enough.

Although I could see his pain I couldn't feel it because I had my own. As a wife I comforted him and promised with the grace of God everything would work out. Keeping the focus on my son was what mattered, not us.

Chapter 32

Nikki

I called Greg once Camille got in the shower. He didn't have a clue who I was, but I told him to trust me because my life was on the line. I told him the situation and that his son was safe. If he tried anything drastic it would backfire. I promised to be in touch and hung up.

I cleared the call, and then I turned the prepaid phone off, and tucked it in a safe spot in Camille's house just in case she started snooping through my things.

I quietly went downstairs to make tea. Later Camille came down with the baby. She wouldn't leave him alone with me for a second, for fear of me running off with him. I asked to hold him and she politely handed him over. "Camille, how old is the baby?" I asked.

She said he had to be around nine weeks. He was so handsome and a happy little fella. Looking at him made me wish my life was in order so that I could have a baby.

"Nikki, don't go getting misty-eyed with the baby," Camille joked.

She knew what I'd been through and I knew what she'd been through. I understood why she took the baby, but it wasn't right. Camille needed a love of her own; someone who would love her unconditionally. Walter did, but Camille's mental disorder and rants drove him into the arms of another woman. I loved her to death, but she needed help.

When the officers arrived with a search warrant, they took out some baby items, which Camille explained she had because she made a gift basket for Greg. They didn't locate the baby or the closet, it was nicely installed and it could not be detected. I wanted to hide, but they searched everywhere preventing me not to and my big ass couldn't fit in that closet with the baby.

I directed my attention back to the baby and he smiled. He was such a cutie.

My cell rang and it was David. I quickly handed Camille back the baby and answered my phone.

"Hello, David," I said.

"Hi, sunshine," he responded. His conversation was like a breath of fresh air. We talked, giggled, and acted like teenagers.

Camille cleared her throat for my attention and I brushed her off. David stated he would be in town this weekend for a workshop and would love to hang out before heading back. I agreed that would work and ended the call.

"Nikki, who is David?" Camille asked, with her nose stuck up.

"The officer that kicked Mike out; we've been having conversations ever since."

"That was quick, it's too soon, Nikki, don't you think?"

"Nope, you worry about this baby, and I'll worry about me," as I sashayed to the kitchen.

"Nikki, can you go to the supermarket and pick up some items? I can order online and you can pick them up in the drive through area, it's convenient," Camille asked.

At first I was hesitant, but decided to go to get out of the house. If I said no, she would put the baby in danger by going herself. Who knows, she would probably try to fit him in her purse for fear of leaving him alone with me. It wouldn't surprise me if she left him alone to run errands.

I took the cash Camille handed me and headed out the door. It was beginning to get cold out, so I bundled up.

When I arrived at the high end supermarket Camille sent me to, the service was great and convenient, as Camille said it would be. I never knew you could grocery shop online. I pulled up to the curb, gave the clerk the order number Camille printed out, and they loaded the items. While sitting in the car, the car behind me hit my bumper. "You've got to be kidding me," I said as I looked through the mirror. I got out of the car, and met the gentleman who hit it. He apologized and accessed the damage.

The clerk offered to call the cops, but the gentleman stated no need, he would handle everything. Noticing the dent I shook my head at the guy, who claimed to have been reaching for his cell phone that fell from his grasp. I reached on the passenger side to get my insurance card from my purse, when I walked back towards the gentleman he asked me, "Where is the baby?"

I realized that this guy followed me from Camille's house.

"Huh?" was all I managed to get out. The guy reached in my bag and pulled out one of the formulas Camille ordered. I quickly paid the clerk and stumbled. "Miss, we need to talk, can you pull over? I will tell you who I am," he said.

Nervous as hell, I decided to pull over. The guy stated he was a friend of Greg's, who mentioned the phone call I made to him. I was hesitant in speaking with him until he explained his connection and how I can help.

"Nikki, you're not in trouble, at least not yet," he said. "Camille is going down and if you don't cooperate, you will too."

This man knew way too much about me. He had a copy of my background record. He knew where I lived, my husband, and where I was employed. I was flabbergasted.

He came up with a plan that would involve me, while keeping me out of jail at the same time by turning Camille in. What was it that I had gotten myself into? I had no clue. I should have stayed back home and dealt with Mike's cheating ass rather than this bullshit.

"Nikki, you have to remain calm, like you know nothing in order for this to work. Now that I know where the baby is, I'll take it from here. If you utter a word, it will cost you."

He said he would get my car fixed; I took his card and hid it, then I quickly drove off watching him in my rear view. I needed a plan to come out of this alive and without anyone getting hurt.

* * *

I pulled in the garage, grabbed the bags, unlocked the door, and jumped when I saw Camille waving a gun.

"Where the hell have you been? What took so long?" she asked demanding answers.

"Camille, get that gun out my face! Traffic was awful, dammit, and some idiot hit my bumper and sped off. I saw Camille running to the car to see if I was lying and came back in.

I was scared, so I didn't move. "Hand over your phone, Nikki," she demanded.

"What? Camille you are paranoid, put the gun down," I yelled.

"Do what I ask Nikki and hand it over!" Camille ordered. She used that gun to keep control.

I stood there in disbelief until I heard the gun go off...POW! All I remember was hitting the floor.

Chapter 33

Camille

The gun went off and shot a hole through the kitchen door that lead to the garage. "Nikki, get your ass off the floor!" I hollered.

. Luckily Nikki had no phone calls except that David guy.

"Camille, put the gun down, now!" Nikki said covering her head.

I did, I felt like I was going crazy and couldn't control myself or trust anyone, not even Nikki. The baby hollered from the top of his lungs, the room was spinning, and I was losing it. I put the gun away and went to attend to the baby.

I rocked Greg but he kept crying. I tried giving him a bottle and a pacifier but he continued to holler. I was irritated and Nikki knew it.

"Camille, let me try. Hand him over."

"Here! This brat is getting on my last damn nerve!"

I handed the baby over and grabbed the phone to call his dad. I went upstairs to get away from the noise and on the second ring, Greg answered.

"Camille,'" he answered.

"Hi, you. I missed you," He was silent on the other end and finally said he missed me, too. I asked to see him, but he kept singing the same tune on how complicated his life was.

"Greg, did you mean what you said when I called your home?"

"No, but I'd rather you not do it again; you are upsetting Michelle."

"Soon, Michelle won't matter," I reminded him. "So, what was the problem?" Greg said she would not give him a divorce if I kept harassing her. She had some nerve. "Why hold on to a man who don't want you?" I asked. "Greg please come over," I begged.

"Camille, it's not that easy. I have people following my every move," Greg whined.

"I need to make a confession, but not over the phone," I said while rolling my eyes, hoping he would buy it.

"Is this your way of getting me to come over?" he asked, trying to brush me off.

I got very heated, "NO!" I yelled. "You need to get over here," I demanded. I was tired of playing games with him. Finally, he agreed it would have to be midnight to dodge a media frenzy.

* * *

I looked around in the closet looking for the perfect outfit; I wanted to have on something nice when Greg arrived. I picked out a lace bikini and matching bra, then pulled down a shoe box containing a pair of studded pumps.

"Camille, come here, the baby has a temperature of 104.3!" Nikki yelled.

I walked downstairs to see what was going on and told her to fix it because his father was coming over later.

"What!" Nikki said like someone was coming to see her big ass.

"Yes, Greg is coming over after midnight," I beamed. I threw her a box of infant Tylenol to give to the baby and left the room.

"Camille, he is really warm, I think he needs to see a doctor," Nikki said, trying to ruin my night.

"Nikki, you know that's not happening, so get him well!"

She shook her head. "What's wrong with you?" she asked. "You're like a person I never knew existed!"

I turned around with tears in my eyes. "I know, Nikki. I know. I feel like I'm losing my mind, but...I'm sure I'll be okay once Greg gets here," I reasoned.

Nikki walked over and tried to hug me, but I pushed her away and headed back upstairs. I didn't need sympathy, I needed Greg!

Chapter 34

Camille

A couple of hours passed and the noise finally subsided. The baby was sleeping; I cleaned and got ready for Greg's arrival. I had Nikki to check in and comfort my son before locking him up until Greg left.

I noticed Nikki staring at me through the mirror as I combed my hair and turned my head.

"Camille, the baby is still not doing well."

"Can you give him more medicine and put a damp towel over his head. I really can't deal with this right now."

Nikki left the room and did as she was told. An hour passed and finally the door bell rang. The baby was finally down and Nikki proceeded to her room. I did a final check and went to let Greg in. We greeted each other and I must say he looked good. He didn't look worried at all.

This was my time to let him know how I really felt about him.

"You look good," I said.

"Yeah, you, too. It's been awhile. So what's up, what did you have to tell me that you couldn't say over the phone?" he said, getting straight to the point.

Greg looked agitated and wouldn't sit. I walked to the kitchen before he could get another word out. I felt his eyes following me.

I returned with two wine glasses and found that he was still standing.

"Greg, please have a seat."

He finally proceeded to the couch and I sat as close as I could next to him. I inhaled his cologne. It did something to me every time; it was always a turn on for me.

"Camille, what's wrong?" Greg asked, sounding nervous.

As bad as I wanted to bring up the search warrant incident, and let him know that I knew of his involvement, I decided to hold off.

"Greg, do you still love me?"

"Yeah," Greg said dry. I knew he was lying.

"So, what's holding you back from us?"

"Camille, for heaven's sake, my son is still missing and I don't know if he's dead or alive. I don't have time for extra curricular activities, what do you really have to tell me?" he said, standing up.

I got up, went in a drawer next to the coffee table, and pulled out a black box. Greg instantly noticed the box and became stiff.

"What's that in your hand, Camille?"

"Open it, you'll see," I said, as I handed Greg the black box. He slowly opened it and looked at me, stunned.

"Greg will you marry me?"

I took his hand and tried to take his wedding band off that he shares with Michelle, but he hesitated at first. Finally he let me slide the ring on his finger.

"Together as one we'll find our son," I said.

"Camille, what is this talk about *our* son? What is this game you're playing?" he asked, getting in my face.

"Babe, when you're with me, what's yours is mine, so technically he will be my son, too. Greg stop worrying so much. He is safe, I know he is," I assured him.

"How do you know that? Is there something you want to tell me?" he yelled.

"Babe, calm down, I'm just trying to make you feel better."

"Camille, I have to go. I don't have time for this charade."

"Greg," I called out. I walked over grabbed his hand and caressed my face with it; he pulled back as I stepped closer. "Greg, kiss me."

He looked at me, pulled the ring off his finger, and said he couldn't marry me because he was already married.

"But you don't love her. The marriage is over. You promised a life with me and led me to believe that we could be together."

"No, Camille, I didn't," Greg responded. "Look, I really have to leave."

"No, you can't leave you just got here; we haven't made love yet, Greg! I wore the perfect bikini, bra, and your favorite dress," I said as I pulled my dress down letting it fall to the floor, hoping that would get him to change his mind.

He turned his head and walked toward the door. "If you walk out that door, you will regret it," I threatened, as I put my dress back on.

"Is that another threat?" He yelled, while walking back toward me. It was as though he wanted to hit me.

"As a matter of fact it is, so help me God."

"You are sick! I didn't know you were so crazy, Camille," he said, leaving walking towards his car.

"Greg, you'll never see your son if you don't come back here, Greg…Greg…Greg, baby, I'm sorry!"

Neighbors ran out to see what was going on. I cried as I kneeled down in the driveway. All I heard were his tires screeching down the street as I tried to gather myself up from the concrete to keep from looking foolish.

Chapter 35

Greg

I drove in anger and cursed all the way home. I was meeting Ed and the detectives at the house. I recorded everything she said and to think she didn't think I heard her in the driveway saying, "I'll never see my son again if I didn't come back," made me nauseous. I knew she had something to do with his disappearance, but the cops didn't find anything during their search only some baby items she claimed were for a gift she was putting together for me. This situation has made me sick; I would kill her if I could get away with it.

What Camille didn't know was that her friend, Nikki, who called me previously to assure me Greg Jr. was safe, was standing at the stairway watching us, then she held up a written sign in big letters when Camille's back was turned that told me my baby was there, that Camille had a gun, and to be careful.

I played it cool and put a finger to my lips, then mouthed the word okay. Her friend stopped watching us briefly, but returned to the stairway when I asked Camille if she was threatening me. That feeling of knowing my son was alive was a relief, but we had to get him out of there as safely as possible. Camille was a crazy psychopath and I never saw that in her, not one sign. "I picked the wrong woman to screw," I thought. Cheating pussy always comes with a price.

Driving frantically, I finally turned in my subdivision and pushed for my garage door to open. I walked in and saw Michelle, Dianne, Ed, my mom, and both detectives, Floyd and Ball, waiting.

"What happened?" Ed asked.

"Craziness, that's what happened! I recorded our conversation; can you believe she asked me to marry her?"

"What? You got involved with a nut case, Greg!" Michelle said hurt; she stormed off, as Dianne followed. My mom was there for support. She listened briefly and said she'll be upstairs praying.

"Ed, man, she has my son. We have to do something quick in case she does something stupid or leaves town with him."

"Greg, she's not going to hurt the baby" Ed said as he listened to the recording. From the sound of it, she wants you. We have to be careful when dealing with a psychopathic killer," Ed said nonchalantly.

"What the hell do you mean a killer, man?"

Ed shared with me the lab report on the exhuming of her ex-husband, Walter. It came back positive for drug poisoning that caused him to have a heart attack at the wheel. The drugs codeine and morphine were found in his system, and when they are mixed together, especially combined with any type of alcohol, it could be deadly.

"Oh, my God!" Michelle said as she wept while listening from the back of the room.

I turned around and noticed everyone had returned. Michelle got even angrier and stated she was giving me twenty-four hours to handle the bitch or she would! She left the room again and this time I went after her.

Dianne stopped me, "Let me handle this, you've done enough," she said. I held my hands up and said, "Fine."

We listened to what each of the detectives had to say about getting another search warrant that would authorize bringing in a K-9 search team and an arrest warrant for her husband's death, but not sure their case against her would hold up in court.

"At this time, Greg, we're not sure if or when she would be arrested for her husband's death, but the District Attorney has her file on his desk right now. We will get a search warrant to search her home again. Don't worry, we also have someone watching the house in case she tries to leave. She won't get far," Detective Ball said.

I was still in shock that this woman poisoned her husband because he was divorcing her for someone else and was now taking it out on me, and my family, because I can't give her what she needs. You can't force anyone to be with you, a reason he probably wanted out of their relationship I bet.

Ed explained the Nikki situation and her willingness to help, but what I couldn't understand was why she didn't just leave unless Camille was threatening her as well. I knew Ed spoke with her at Publix after he followed her leaving Camille's house, but I'm not sure he spoke to her after that.

I sat quietly when Detective Floyd asked me if I was telling them everything about my involvement with Camille. I looked at him with disgust on my face ignoring his question.

"I'm sorry Greg, I'm just asking. We are indeed focusing on what we have, and Camille's involvement. I just want to make sure there are no surprises later into the investigation" Detective Floyd stated.

"Neither my wife nor I have anything to hide. This woman has terrorized my family and she still hasn't been arrested for attacking my wife." I was getting upset because I felt like they were taking their time with this matter.

"Greg, calm down. You know it's standard procedure," Ed said as he pulled me away from my seat. "Don't let them get to you, man!"

It's 2 a.m. and we were still talking. Detective Floyd kept looking at me like he hated my guts for some reason.

"Greg, because of men like you it's hard for brothers like me to find a decent woman!" he blurted.

"Excuse me? Get the fuck out of my house both of you!" I said. I started walking toward him; Ed grabbed me and told me to have a seat. I almost snapped and that's what he wanted.

I told Ed to make sure they leave and don't come back; they were not helping the situation.

They both left with no hesitation and said they'd be in touch. I walked out of the room and looked for Michelle, when suddenly I heard the garage door open and saw Michelle pull out of the driveway. I went to the door, "Michelle! Michelle!" I called out. She headed down the street like a bat out of hell.

I turned around and saw my mom standing there holding out her arms. I fell in and cried. We prayed together and she promised the good Lord would take care of us and bring Jr. home. Her faith was the only thing getting her through this ordeal.

"Mom, I didn't mean to hurt anyone or for this to happen," I said breaking down in front of her.

"I know, son, I know. We all make some bad choices in life; we have to fix it. But the first step is getting my grandson back safe and sound," she said. I could always count on my mom for support no matter what the situation was, good or bad.

As we talked, Dianne ran downstairs screaming, "Michelle is gone! I thought she was in the bathroom…"

"Calm down, Dianne, I saw her leave and thought you were with her," I said.

"Oh no! We have to get to Camille's house. Michelle has a gun and she's not in her right mind," Dianne said, sounding so sure of herself.

I jumped over the couch, told mom to stay put, called out for Ed, grabbed the keys, and left.

Chapter 36

Michelle

I was determined to get my baby back from this fool by any means necessary. I wasn't going to sit around and wait for the cops to handle it; I was going to handle it myself! While riding all I could think about was my baby, I called my mom and cried non-stop as I drove. She kept telling me not to do anything drastic. My other line kept beeping one call after the other. I knew it was Dianne or Greg, but I kept driving. I told my mom I'd call her back, she tried desperately to keep me on the phone. My head throbbed as I tried to make sense of the situation.

"Was I not good enough?" I kept asking myself. "What was it, Greg?" I couldn't understand why he did what he did and how his problem became our problem. I felt so betrayed and so little that I didn't even know him. I was talking to myself non-stop, ignoring all incoming calls. My mind went everywhere and the thoughts I had were not good.

I changed into all black gear, ready for war wearing a hoodie, sneakers, and sweat pants. I had to pull myself together before I dealt with this crazy broad. I circled around Camille's neighborhood to check it out before parking, and saw a guy sitting in a parked car. He was probably the one watching her house, he looked to be asleep. I drove around the block and parked in between two cars that were parked outside the curb.

The way I was feeling I could see how so many women ended up on the TV show "Snapped!" I was at my breaking point. I got out quietly, looked around, made sure my phone was on silent and that my gun was loaded and tucked in the back of my sweats. I walked fast trying to hurry but not wanting to look suspicious. I heard barking then realized I had to jump the same fence as before. My ankle and leg were still sore from the previous episode.

Thank you! The man sitting in the parked car finally left his spot hopefully making a coffee run. I saw a light on in Camille's house and walked to the front door. With my heart racing and sweat running from my forehead, I rang the door bell, and then knocked frantically for her to open up.

I heard commotion inside before someone asked, "Who is beating on my door like that!"

"Camille, this is Michelle, open up!" I demanded.

"Michelle?"

"Dammit, Camille, don't play games with me, open this damn door before I kick it in!" I yelled.

The door opened slowly. I put my hand on my gun just in case she tried something stupid. There stood a woman with brown skin, medium length hair, and a mole right on her chin as I recalled during the attack. I gasped when I realized it was her who attacked me. She smirked, then opened her mouth, "Michelle, what can I do for you at this hour? If you're looking for Greg he isn't here."

"Tramp, don't try me!" I said, as I pushed past her and made my way through her home the same way she invaded my privacy. I looked around her house like a deranged woman stalking her prey. She stood watching as I tore her house up.

"Camille, where is he? Where's my son, dammit!" The smirk on her face sickened me. She walked towards me.

"I don't know where he is, Michelle. But did you know that Greg and I are getting married as soon as you release him from your clutches?"

She had to be the sickest woman I had ever come into contact with.

"You sound pathetic!" I said, laughing in her face. "Nobody is going to marry a woman who poisoned her own husband, and if somebody is stupid enough to marry you, they'll leave just like he tried to.

Her eyes grew big knowing her secret was out.

"No one poisoned Walter and for you to barge into my home talking ridiculous is so like you!"

"Did you know his body was exhumed?"

"You are now making up shit! I know you are trying to ruin my life because of Greg's affair with me. Michelle, I'm sorry that your son is still missing, but please don't come here bringing me your problems."

"You are really delusional! You want my life so bad that you would attack me and kidnap my son because you can't have kids and to think you and Greg will be a family…" I laughed at her, I told her she would never be a mom; she couldn't be a wife because she killed her first husband and nobody wants a lunatic. Camille became speechless and I could tell I was getting under her skin; it was just a matter of time before she exploded.

"Yeah, I read the reports and spoke to your physician. I know all about you, Camille from Ashe, North Carolina."

"What report!" she hollered. I could tell she was getting agitated and was blowing steam by her tone but, I didn't back down.

"The reports were from the excavation of Walter's body for testing and they indicated he was positive for codeine and morphine poisoning, so your two year run is over dear."

"Oh no," a lady gasp from the stairway looking concerned.

"Who are you?" I looked up and asked.

"Nikki," she said. Something about her didn't set well with me; she had a concerned look on her face.

"Camille, I need you upstairs now," Nikki said speaking softly and shaking.

I observed their eye contact and the way Nikki was shaking. It was obvious that something was wrong. Camille stood there; I finally jetted up the stairway with Camille right behind me. She managed to grab my leg and pull me back down. I turned around on my back and kicked her in the face as she stumbled down the steps.

"The baby is not breathing," Nikki screamed from the stairway.

"NO!" I screamed. I grabbed the rail, headed back up the stairs, when all of a sudden shots rang out. One hit me in the leg on the opposite side. I saw blood run down my leg but didn't care at the moment. I got up for the sake of my baby.

Suddenly there was banging on the door and when I looked up, I saw Nikki holding my baby. "Nikki, run," Camille said…"put him back, now!" She hollered.

There was banging at the door. "Open up! Camille…open the door!" We struggled on the stairway. Camille tried to get past me to get to the baby, but I blocked her off.

"Camille!" Nikki screamed. "I think he's dead!"

"He's not dead, that can't be," I managed to say, as I reached the top of the stairway. "Hand him over!" I demanded.

"Don't you dare move, Nikki! She's not the one calling the shots!" Camille fired back.

"Nikki, you need to call 911!" I said.

Camille tried to take him out of her arms; I walked towards her with my gun. "Don't you dare touch him!" I said.

Camille turned around, then back at Nikki, next thing I knew Camille charged me and we found ourselves tossing with the gun. Nikki ran past us both and down the stairs with the baby.

"Michelle!" someone called out.

"I'm up here!" Several shots went into the ceiling when we stumbled down the steps with her landing on top of me trying to grab the gun.

She fell over from Greg kicking her in the side, he pulled me up, and I quickly ran to my baby. Dianne was there. She had taken him away from Nikki and started giving him CPR.

"He has a pulse," Dianne said nervously.

"Thank God!" I said, crying hysterically. Nikki stood over us apologizing and rambling about what happened while we waited on the paramedics. Greg ran over to assist us while the baby gasped for air, I was shaking and nervous all at once.

"Thank you for your help, Nikki. You did great!" Greg offered.

Then the unthinkable happened.

Suddenly we heard a shot fired. Camille had managed to get up and had grabbed her gun and shot Greg in the back. Then she turned her attention to Nikki, "You were helping them, huh? You bitch, you were my friend!" she screamed.

"Camille, I'm sorry! I just called him when Michelle arrived, I promise."

"I don't believe you!" she yelled, as she shot Nikki.

I watched Greg but knew better than to move. Camille waved the gun back and forth from Dianne to me.

"Please put the gun down, Camille," Dianne pleaded. "Please! Before something terrible happens!"

I watched in agony, as sirens neared. I was terrified as I watched my baby trying to breathe. I was determined to no longer be victimized by this woman. I needed to get my baby out of there.

Before I knew it, I charged her like a bull. I was enraged as we wrestled with the gun; she kicked me in the abdomen still holding onto the gun.

Both hands were in the air with her still holding onto the gun shooting into the ceiling. I managed to elbow her in the jaw, knocking the gun from her hand. We both crawled, trying to get it. I grabbed it, turned around, and shot her right in the chest causing her to hit her head on the end table. Camille fell over and that was it. I panicked; sweat ran down like pouring water.

"Greg!" Ed called. But although he was breathing, he was unresponsive. The same look for Nikki, who was also unresponsive.

The paramedics came and began working on Greg Jr., who finally broke out with a tiny cry! It was the best feeling in the world.

Once I knew my baby was okay, I ran to Greg and called his name out several times, but nothing. The paramedics put him on a stretcher, and then Nikki. I watched helplessly as they tried to get him to respond.

At that moment I had no control over anything; not my son, husband, or my emotions. I jumped in the ambulance with Jr., and Ed went along with Greg. This situation was really testing my faith, I thought.

Chapter 37

Nikki

I woke up and couldn't remember anything or where I was. There were machines, needles, and nurses everywhere. Mike was also in the room, and standing over me.

"She's awake," I heard someone say.

He kissed my cheek. A tear ran down my face. I couldn't move and was in excruciating pain. He explained that I had been shot and had been unconscious for a good while, and that I had just come out of surgery.

The doctor came into the room as Mike stood nearby. "Nikki my dear, you're still in danger because of the way the bullet went into your chest, and struck a lung causing it to rupture," the doctor stated. "I will keep a close watch on you and perform a series of tests to get you well." he added.

As he was talking, I started remembering what had taken place, and I tried talking, but couldn't. At the same time, the doctor attempted to ask me do I remember anything. When I couldn't answer, he instructed me to blink one time for yes and two times for no.

Afterwards, I signaled for Mike to bring me paper and a pen. I scribbled "Camille did it." Tears ran down my face as I recalled my best friend trying to kill me.

Mike shook his head and squeezed my hand, "I know, sweetheart, I know."

As I looked around, I saw other familiar faces like my neighbor, Mary, my niece, and my brother who all flew in I suppose to be by my side. I was heavily sedated. I jotted down words and asked about Camille. Mike stated she is in a coma and not to worry about her. I assured him that I forgave her on paper. Mike took the paper and wrote back that he loved me; I looked at him in tears. He wiped them as they fell down my face.

Ed walked in with a detective. I had to answer more questions regarding Camille and the kidnapping. I was forced to answer questions by using blinking signals.

"Well," Ed started. "The good news is that you're not in any trouble. But the bad news is that you could be under fire for not turning Camille in. I'm sorry that things happened this way."

I blinked as he spoke. I knew he was apologetic, but it wasn't his fault, it was Camille's.

Ed also thanked me for my help as he talked briefly with Mike and the doctors, moments later both men exited the room. I couldn't believe Camille, the friend I trusted with my life, would shoot me. I said a prayer that God remove that evil spirit from her. With all that has happened, I didn't know if I deserved a second chance at life. I could have done something before this situation got out of hand, but I didn't.

My brother started talking to me and massaging my hands when all of a sudden I started coughing real heavy, coughing up blood. It got so bad the nurse was called in and she paged "code green to room 246." My lung was collapsing due to the bullet wound. I couldn't breathe; the doctors ran in and put a mask over my face for oxygen. I struggled to hang on and tried desperately, suddenly my body went into shock while I fought to breathe.

"Please leave the room," the nurse ordered everyone.

"No, I won't leave her here by herself," Mike shouted.

I glanced at my brother, as I was in and out of consciousness. Mike wouldn't leave the room and was forced out. At that moment everything became a blur. I shook, my lungs swelled, and I bled internally, drowning in my own blood. The doctor yelled for me to be wheeled into surgery immediately, before I could make it to surgery my vision became less and my system completely shut down.

Chapter 38

Greg

I was lucky that the bullet didn't graze my spine; it missed it by one centimeter. Although I was still in bad condition from the gunshot to the back, I tried to remain positive. That single bullet still did a lot of damage. The bullet went in beside my kidney, clipped off the tip of my heart, causing it to collapse, barely missed my spine, which spared me from paralysis and death.

I looked around the room and saw my mom; she smiled when I looked up. The door opened and Michelle walked in with a cast on her leg and with Greg Jr. I cried with tears of joy knowing he was not harmed and in good health. I couldn't remember everything from the ordeal but when I saw how big and handsome he was, I didn't care. He was every bit of twelve weeks. His smile was to die for.

"Hi, you," Michelle said.

"Hi," I mumbled. I was so sedated; I was in and out, mouth dry and sore.

Mom walked over and gave me water. She then left the room to give us some privacy.

"Michelle, I'm sorry about everything," I managed to say. She put her finger over my lips for me to be quiet. I watched her with the baby and knew she was going to be a great mom. She limped across the room, but looked so happy and I was happy to have our son back. They were my world.

"Camille." Michelle hesitated at first but stated she was in a coma. My thought was, "She's not dead yet?" I glanced out the window trying to recall the entire episode. Then Ed walked into the room.

"Hey, partner, glad to see you awake!" he said. I smiled but stated I was still sore.

Michelle filled Ed in on what the doctors said – I should make a full recovery although I'm under observation from the bullet wound and was still in bad shape. Ed shared with us that he was just informed that Nikki had died from her injuries shortly after he left her room.

"Oh no," Michelle said in agony while covering her mouth. "The wrong woman just died!" she hollered.

"Michelle, I know how you feel," Ed said. He also shared with us that they did a complete search of Camille's home and got a tip from a guy who noticed Camille's picture from the news that linked her to the kidnapping. He contacted the police last night that he and some guys did some work at her house and installed a soundproof closet in her bedroom closet. Lo and behold that's where she kept the baby all that time. "Only the K-9 unit would have detected that," he said.

"'That son of a bitch did what?" Michelle yelled, scaring the baby.

"Calm down, Michelle," Ed asked of her.

Michelle was even more upset, I tried to sit up after hearing that information, then my IV came out. Ed paged the nurse, who came back in and told me not to move much. She inserted the IV back in and left.

We also found out Camille kept all the baby items in that same closet, so when we went there to check the place out, it was all put away. She was very clever. I knew all along she played a part in the kidnapping, but I praise Nikki for contacting me. I was distraught that Nikki lost her life and I blamed myself.

Ed took the baby from Michelle's arm and I noticed how Michelle watched Ed hold Jr. as he smiled from ear to ear, not letting him out her sight. With all that Michelle has been through, she was on edge concerning our son. I'm not sure if she can ever forgive me or if our marriage will survive. I wouldn't blame her if she left.

"Man, he has feet like you," Ed joked.

I managed to laugh, but kept coughing. We all were so busy admiring the baby that I didn't notice Michelle's parents had walked in.

Ed excused himself and said he'd check back in a couple of hours. I just knew this visit was going to be bad. Michelle's father was always protective of her. Both of them embraced their daughter and awed over the baby. They all cried with joy that this nightmare was finally over, then her dad Charles stood with his hands in his pocket and looked at me in disgust. He walked over, "Hello, Greg."

"Hello, Pops," I managed to say.

"It's Charles to you," he snapped back.

"Honey, not now," Susan said. She walked over trying to pull him away.

"Please, excuse us, I need to talk to Greg," Charles said.

I knew he hated my guts, but I wasn't in the mood for any more negativity unless it came from Michelle. I always admire Charles and the way he treated Susan. He was a real man and I didn't live up to his expectations for his daughter.

I pushed the bed upwards, so I could sit up straight.

"Greg this ordeal has really taken a toll on my daughter and my entire family. You put your family in grave danger and almost lost my grandson forever, not to forget Michelle's ordeal from being attack from the same woman who put you in this hospital bed."

"All I can do is apologize Charles, I'm sorry. I've assessed this situation over and over and pray that Michelle will forgive me in due time."

"Greg, you never know how a person is and a reason you got married was not to find out."

"You are so right. I can't change what has happened, but I'm glad my son is home safe. I hope you can see it in your heart to forgive me as well, Charles. I made a mistake."

It was useless to say anymore, I figured I would give everyone time.

He got up and started walking.

"Charles," I called out. He turned around and I told him how much I respected him and that I didn't mean to hurt anyone. Charles turned back around and walked out the door not saying a word.

Susan came in next. She stood in front of the bed and wiped away tears, "You know you really hurt my daughter and our grandson. Was Michelle not enough Greg?" Susan looked away and then continued, "I'm going to be brief, you know what you did, but we have to learn to forgive. You put your family in grave danger, whatever the future holds, it will be," she added.

Susan looked back and saw Michelle standing behind her; she embraced her mom and kissed her on the cheek. Susan left the room to spend time with the baby.

"I hope my father wasn't too harsh," Michelle said.

"Not that harsh, but do you blame him? If I had a daughter I would be the same way."

I looked at her, grabbed her hand, "Do you still love me, Michelle?"

"Greg, I do and always will; but right now our future is bleak."

"There is a long road ahead, and I will do whatever it takes to keep my family," I said reaching out for her hand.

I told Michelle my feelings and thoughts. We both held hands and cried. She didn't say much and I wondered what she was thinking. I knew she loved me, but is that enough to stay? I wondered.

She was my rock; I got caught up in my thoughts and didn't realize Michelle had left the room. The phone rang and I struggled to pick it up, I heard a rhapsody weak voice on the other end, "Hello, Greg," the woman said. Then I realized it was Camille.

I screamed through the phone for her ass not to call me ever again and looked up to find Charles standing at the door.

"Was that your mistress?" Charles asked.

Chapter 39

Camille

I finally regained consciousness from a coma. I had been shot and the bullet missed my lung by an inch and did not hit a single vital organ. But the head injuries I sustained from the coffee table gave me cerebral hemorrhage. The fall, along with the gunshot wound, made me lose a lot of blood.

I looked around trying to remember everything. I called Greg's room after hearing one of the men outside the room discussing him. He cursed me and was very cruel, I was puzzled.

I got out the bed and every alarm in the room went off. My head was spinning. A nurse ran in and told me to get back in bed, cops swarmed the place all over. "Was I in danger?" I asked. The nurse called for the doctor who came in and checked me. He went out of the room and called a cop who came in and read me my rights. All I heard was murder, kidnapping, endangering a child, weapons charges, and the list went on. I laughed at the cop and told him he had the wrong person. He immediately handcuffed my hands to the bed.

"Let me out of here!" I said, as I kicked and screamed. "Get these cuffs off of me, you're hurting me!" I yelled.

"I need to see my husband, he's in room 223, Greg Langston. Call him, he will tell you the truth!" A team of doctors came in and strapped me to the bed to where I couldn't move. "Please, can somebody let me know what's going on?" I asked.

One of the doctors signaled for everyone to leave and to speak to me alone. Once alone I asked him was everything okay. Looking at some images of what looked like X-rays, he asked me if I recalled anything that happened. I told him I remember getting into an altercation with my husband's girlfriend, I remembered struggling over a gun, and I remembered falling into a coffee table and hitting my head.

"What about the baby?" he asked.

"What baby?"

"The one you kidnapped?"

I was stunned. "No one kidnapped a baby. I remember Greg giving me his son because Michelle wasn't able to see about him," I told the doctor, and he quickly jotted down notes. Another doctor and nurse walked in and evaluated the session I guess.

"What about your friend, Nikki, where is she?" he asked me more questions.

"I don't know, she was at my house when Michelle and I got into it."

"Camille, Nikki died a short while ago; you killed her," Doctor Reese said.

My eyes became large as I tried to get up, "You're lying. I didn't kill her! She's my best friend! Where is she?" I asked.

Both doctors looked at each other and left the room. The nurse stayed behind while she sedated my IV once more.

I laughed when the door shut. These mutherfuckers will think I'm crazy before they send me to lock up. I will plead insane before I go to jail.

I remember everything and Nikki's ass deserved what she got, she betrayed me. Nikki knew what she was doing by bringing the baby out for Michelle to see him, talking about he wasn't breathing. I didn't mean to shoot her. Before I knew it, I pulled the trigger. I really felt sorry, but she deserved it. Now Nikki will learn to keep her mouth shut, forever!

I really needed to find out about Michelle, "She tried to kill me and it ain't over yet," I mumbled.

Doctor Reese returned with Doctor Wang who both stated I have memory loss or what they call "amnesia," a condition in which the head injuries I sustained could be permanent or temporary. They will have to evaluate and do more testing.

"Memory loss," I just told you what I remembered Doctor Reese!"

"Camille, you are unable to recall past events and what you're recalling is not what happened!" he said.

A cop came in along with Ed's ass and the District Attorney who all stood in the back.

"Camille, do you recognize this guy?" pointing to Ed.

"Why, yes, that's my husband's best friend. He was the best man at our wedding. Edward, please tell them I'm okay."

He just stood there and looked around and as bad as I wanted to laugh, I kept a straight face.

I was hit with more questions that I didn't answer to their liking. The District Attorney went over all the things I did and how I cost tax payers a lot of money by kidnapping someone's child while everyone was out searching for a baby that didn't turn up. How I used Nikki as a bandit who tried reluctantly but failed in trying to get me to return the baby, but lost her life in the end. He went on and on that I've had enough.

"You're lying; I didn't do those things!" I yelled at them.

"What about your husband, Walter, who you poisoned?" the District Attorney asked.

"Don't talk about my deceased husband, you're lying. All of you are lying. Please go get my husband! Please!" I screamed to the top of my lungs but couldn't move.

I noticed Doctor Wang signaled for everyone to leave the room. Doctor Reese came over and injected my IV with a needle – whatever was in it calmed me as I began to zone out.

Chapter 40

Ed

We all left the room to discuss Camille. Nothing about her spoke the truth and I told the District Attorney, as much. I had seen her type of behavior before. I knew that she was acting.

Although it was confirmed that she had bipolar disorder, she knew what she was doing and it wouldn't work.

Dr. Reese and Dr. Wang both walked into the conference room with paperwork. They went over her x-rays, which revealed trauma to the right side of her head causing memory loss along with blood loss, from the bullet wound. Although she may gradually regain it back, it was just a matter of when, Dr. Reese detailed.

"Camille is not stable, which we all know, but I do think she could survive prison, Dr. Wang."

"Doctor, speaking as an attorney, most people in her position will plead insanity," I added. I also explained to him that this was just a cover up. Her ass belonged behind bars, but instead they wanted to send her to a care facility. I knew she understood the nature of her actions; this mental act was a ploy to stay out of jail.

The District Attorney intervened and stated that they have to prove that Camille is and was insane when those crimes took place and that they couldn't do. The only thing they have is memory loss. If a jury considered her insane, then this means Camille would not be responsible for the crimes she committed because of her state of mind.

I do agree that she has a mental disorder that caused her to commit such crimes, but to get away with it and be sent to a facility would not fly with me. How can I explain this to Michelle and Greg?

The District Attorney mentioned a "temporary insanity" plea, which allowed Camille to claim to have been suffering from an irresistible impulse when she attacked Michelle, kidnapped the baby, and poisoned Walter, but is now sane. This means Camille could be released immediately, rather than being incarcerated for psychiatric treatment.

"What about extreme emotional disturbance?" I asked.

"It's a possibility," Dr. Reese stated. "I know she wasn't thinking rationally," he said.

"Yeah, even with that she could be guilty of a lesser crime," I said as I shook my head in disbelief.

"Right now we will keep her under observation, watch her on the monitors, seek psychiatric treatment, and do more testing to make a final ruling for our report," both doctors added.

We all left the room and I talked to the District Attorney about his perspective, because I knew he was determined to prosecute her. I was on board, but that would be hard if the doctors, psychiatrist, and other reports find her insane.

"That's just pure bullshit!" I saw right through her act.

* * *

I returned to Greg's room and greeted him and the room of visitors. I talked to Mom Dukes briefly (Greg's mom as I called her) and grabbed Michelle so I could hold my god son. Dianne stopped by and pulled Michelle to the side, not sure what they discussed, but it looked intense.

I know if anything, all the pain that Greg was in, he would think twice before cheating with somebody he knew nothing about. People are crazy nowadays.

"Greg I need to speak with you and Michelle, alone."

"What is it man, it seems serious?"

"I need to discuss something, with the both of you."

Michelle finally came over, as everyone else exited the room. Susan took the baby along with her.

"I'm sorry I want to talk about Camille" I said.

"Not now Ed, please," Michelle stressed.

"You really need to hear this," I said raising a brow. Both of them looked at each other concerned.

"I just wanted you both to know I just left a meeting at the other end of the hospital where Camille is being held. She is conscious and from the looks of things she's going to be okay."

"What! She's not dead?" Michelle said in fear.

"Baby, please let him finish," Greg said.

The look on Michelle's face showed how displeased she was with the interruption.

"I sat in on a session…with Camille and her doctors because apparently she has amnesia – or memory loss – and was playing the insane card." I went on to explain that the doctors have to prove she's insane in order for her to go to a care facility, this way she won't get any jail time for the crimes she committed.

"Wait a damn minute," Greg interrupted. "You mean to tell me…" he attempted, through coughs, "that she may get off by acting like she's insane?"

"I'm afraid so. I'm doing my best to prove them wrong. I can to make sure this doesn't happen. Neither the District Attorney nor I agree with the doctors, they clearly think she has a mental disorder. I know that she knows what she's doing."

Michelle limped around the room mumbling she should have made sure she was dead, "I tell you this, she comes after my family again this time she will be DOA and I mean it Ed!"

Michelle's mom walked in and asked, "What is it?"

"Mom please give us a minute" Michelle said.

I wasn't happy about the situation just as they weren't. I tried to assure them that this may not happen at all, but wanted them to be aware of what was going on. I plan to make sure Camille gets what she deserves.

"This problem will not go away will it?" Greg said in anger.

"It will," I said.

The District Attorney…is moving forward with prosecuting the case against Camille who wouldn't be evaluated for long because she would eventually slip up.

"So that bullet did nothing to her?" Michelle asked.

"Missed her lung by an inch, the only reason she was in a coma was due to the head trauma she suffered when she hit her head on the coffee table," I said.

I noticed Michelle was shaking, she started talking to herself, then left the room abruptly. I went to the door and called out for her. Michelle's dad noticed, and then followed her; I just hope he got to her in time because her mindset was out for blood.

I watched Greg, who was more than angry and he should be. I walked toward the door, looked back, and said "Greg, that tramp won't get loose, not again, not on my watch," then I shut the door behind me.

Chapter 41

Michelle

I had to leave the room quickly. I thought I was going to suffocate after what I just heard. After what I've just been through, I was going to explode. I limped trying to get to the other end of the building; before I could turn the corner I heard a voice, "Baby girl."

I turned around, "Daddy!"

"Baby girl, come here. You already have one bad leg," he joked.

My dad always had a way of making me feel better, no matter how old I got. I couldn't hold back the tears and cried in his arms as he held them out for me. We walked to an area to talk.

We went in a lounging area and luckily no one was in there. I broke down and told my dad that I did not understand how things got to this place. I shared with him what Ed just told us and that justice had to be served or I would take matters into my own hands and finish the job myself!

"Michelle, baby, please that's not the answer, and don't talk like that."

I looked at him and wondered how someone could just snap. I had totally lost it. If Camille came at me again, I would really kill her.

"Baby girl," he said, looking at me. I have some connections and favors I can collect. I will make sure she gets put behind bars for a very long time. She was sane then and she's sane now!"

"Dad, I need to see her," I said, as he looked at me incredulously.

I limped over to the soda machine, putting pressure on my leg. "Dad, I just need to see what kind of games she's playing, maybe I can get her to break."

"I really don't think that's a good idea."

He offered to take Greg Jr. back home with him and mom so I could get myself together and figure out what Greg and I were going to do about our marriage. Better yet, he preferred I come back with them, but running away wasn't the answer.

"I'll give it some thought," was all I said. We left to go back and I stopped, looked at my dad, and told him "I'll be there shortly; there was something I needed to do." He let out a deep sigh; I turned back around and went in the opposite direction. I left my dad standing there, but felt him watching me along the way.

* * *

I went to wing B on the other end of the hospital where Camille was being held. They said no visitors were allowed, but I pleaded with the receptionist to let me see her, I wasn't taking no for an answer.

I noticed District Attorney Brown talking to a doctor and approached him. "Excuse me, gentlemen, I would like to speak to the District Attorney briefly, please," I said.

They all looked at me, as he led me to the side for some privacy. "What can I do for you?" he asked.

"Thank you for your time. I'm Michelle. Ed stated you are in the process of trying to prosecute Camille, I'm the one whose baby she kidnapped." I then went on to explain what I needed to do.

"I'm familiar with the case, but I'm not sure if it is a good idea to see Camille." He told me to stay put that he would speak with her doctors.

I waited for awhile, but it felt like forever. Finally, a doctor and the District Attorney walked over to me, the doctor explained that he was afraid I could upset Camille. Although they removed the straps from her legs and she's still handcuffed to the bed, seeing me could push her over the edge.

The DA's argument with the doctor was that it might be a good idea to see Camille's reaction, to see if Michelle brings back her memory. They could use this as a session while they watched her behavior on the monitor.

"Five minutes," the doctor finally agreed.

The officer who stood at the door let me in. I didn't know what to expect, but went in and looked at her pathetic ass.

"Camille," I called out. She sat up and stared at me.

"Remember me?"

"Michelle, what a surprise, what brings you by? You want to visit with the baby, today?" Camille asked, acting stupid.

I looked at my victimizer and yelled at her, "Drop the act!"

She looked at me acting all confused; she talked about how I'm still mad because Greg left me and married her. Then she went on to say I should have been a good wife to him; everything she said were the words of a crazy person, but I knew what she was trying to do.

"Camille, cut it out dammit! You are ridiculous; you came into my home, attacked me, took my son, and had him hidden in some closet like an animal. I hope you rot in hell! You are more sick than anything that's walking, you crazy psycho bitch!" I said trying to calm my nerves, but it just wasn't happening.

She was really getting agitated and tried to get out those handcuffs.

"I should have killed you and then we wouldn't be going through this bullshit! Yeah, I said it, "I should have killed you!" Camille said with a grin on her face.

I walked over to her. She tried to kick me; I knew she was being watched. I didn't do what I wanted to do to her ass, instead I got in her face and told her Greg was still married to me and that she was still alone. No Walter, no Greg, no one! Then I spat in my face.

She began acting hysterically, even to the point of singing and balling up in fetal position.

I smirked, watched her for a moment from the door then left the room as if she never existed.

Chapter 42

Michelle

I sat at my table and enjoyed a strong cup of coffee, something I hadn't been able to do in a very long time. My mom and dad had been staying with me to help out with the baby. Greg was finally stable, and would be home soon.

My parents wanted to take the baby with them until things died down, and I had agreed that it was best—at least for a couple of weeks. The pediatrician also thought it would be a good idea to be in a calm surrounding. That way, I could sort things out and heal properly myself.

Days passed since my encounter with Camille. I stayed in touch with the District Attorney who assured me Camille was going to lock up. Although she would be in a padded cell, the doctors still don't think she will be able to function with others as they are trying to move her to a care facility. I felt like I had to watch my back at all times knowing she's not locked away somewhere.

I glanced out the window and knew once Greg got home, we had to talk about us. I dwelled on the situation, but had to make a decision about my future with him.

Dianne walked over and interrupted my thoughts. She was one of the best friends anyone could ever have. Someone like her who drops everything to be with you during good and bad times is a keeper.

She sat, we talked, and then she asked me about Greg and gave her honest opinion about the situation and what she would do, but at that moment I knew I still loved him. I looked at Dianne and said, "Honestly, I would like to start over."

It's hard to just walk away, easier for most, but I've built a life with this man that I don't know if I can give it all up! When it came to love, I loved hard. Although Greg betrayed me, and even put my life and his son's life in danger, I still had an obligation to take care of him.

My mom came into the kitchen to let me know that Detective Floyd was at the door. He stopped by to see the baby and to tell me how much he has prayed for his return.

"You look great, Michelle." he said.

"Thank you!"

Why the hell was I blushing? Detective Floyd wasn't bad looking at all. I guess I really never looked at him in that way. I had too much going on to think about any man including my own.

Mom brought the baby to the door for a brief moment. "Thank you for dropping by Detective," I said. "And by the way thanks for working diligently on the case," I added.

He smiled. "Call if you need anything, you have my card," he said, as he turned to leave.

I called Greg on video chat so that he could say goodbye to the baby. He didn't agree with my decision, but at that moment I was calling the shots.

After everyone left, including Dianne, I was finally alone with my thoughts. Greg called me back, as I ignored the call.

It was still early; I decided to call Detective Floyd at least he was someone I could talk to.

"Detective. Hi, this is Michelle calling."

"What a surprise! What did I do to deserve this call so soon?"

"I was sitting here bored, feeling down on myself."

"Stop, just stop it, you shouldn't be feeling anything, would you like to talk about it?" I was hesitant, but told him yes and if he liked he could come over. His shift was over so he was heading my way.

I went to wash up and to look somewhat presentable when the man came over because I have been looking like hell lately. When the doorbell rang, I knew Detective Floyd had arrived.

"Hi, Detective Floyd," I greeted.

"Oh, we don't need to be so formal. You can call me, Carlos."

He had changed out his uniform and had on regular clothes. He looked great.

"Okay, Carlos," I said smiling.

"Hi, I see you got rid of everyone," he commented.

"Yeah, everyone went home, my mom and dad took the baby back with them."

"And Greg?" he asked, looking around.

"He'll be home tomorrow, I think."

We had good conversation. I ordered pizza, he had a beer and I had a soda since I was taking prescription meds for my leg still. His company was refreshing, just what I needed.

We talked about everything. He told me that he was once married, but his wife left him for someone who had more money. He also told me that the relationship didn't work out and she tried to come back, but he didn't take her back.

He was quiet. I could tell that he wanted to ask me something. Then when he finally spoke, I realized why he had hesitated. "Why are you putting up with that?" he asked. "The cheating, I mean."

"Not sure, I'm just now having time to think."

"You're beautiful inside and out, I don't understand some men," he said, shaking his head.

The conversation turned up a notch; we discussed everything from what he wanted in a woman to our sex lives. At first I was uncomfortable, but he made me feel comfortable in talking to him. The more he talked the more I wanted to get close to him. I felt a connection. I eased in and caressed his face, and then we kissed.

"Let's take this upstairs," I whispered to him.

He picked me up, as I led him upstairs, then he gently laid me down on the bed. I sat up, took his shirt off, and unbuckled his pants, "Hot damn!"

"What is it?" Carlos asked, looking at my facial expression.

"Nothing," I said. This man has the biggest dick I have ever seen I thought, even Greg didn't compare to him and I thought *he* was big.

He undressed me and looked at me, I felt so ashamed I wanted to cover myself up. I have not been with anyone since Greg, it felt awkward, but I didn't care. He kissed me with passion, caressed me, licked me, and went down, and made love to me. Boy, did he feel good; he looked me in my eyes and entered me slowly. His love making was different, and I enjoyed every bit of it.

We both moaned and groaned, took turns at pleasing each other. I went down on him, playfully sucked his balls, then came up for air, and kissed him hard, he flipped me over, squeezed my ass, and took each of my breasts in his mouth. At that moment I wanted to cry, not sure why, but I just did, until I glanced at the monitor and saw a car pull up.

"Holy shit," I said to myself that's Ed with Greg. I paused, but didn't do anything, I continued with Carlos, I got under the sheets and got on top of him. I glided on him like I was ice skating and we both came together. I continued on top of Carlos, he pulled the sheets back where my back and ass were exposed as I sat on him, he fondled me, then all hell broke loose when I heard Greg scream, "MICHELLLLE!!!"

Chapter 43

Greg

I walked into the bedroom and couldn't believe what I was witnessing; Michelle in our bed on top of that slimy Detective.

"Get your ass out of my house now! You son of a bitch! When I get to you, you better hope you're still breathing," I said. "I will have your ass fired!" I told him. He had a smirk on his face, grabbed his things, and left.

Ed walked behind him downstairs to make sure he was leaving. I was so embarrassed I couldn't think straight. I stepped out into the hallway and asked Ed to leave so I could talk with Michelle.

I returned to her, and was bent over in pain from the injuries and my wife's infidelity. "I didn't know you would be home so soon," she said, on her way out the shower.

"So that gives you a reason to have a screw party, while I'm not here?"

She was nonchalant, it didn't bother her a bit that she hurt me.

I looked at her in disgust. "I can't believe you were fucking that man in our bed? How could you, Michelle?" I said raising my voice at her.

She looked at me and laughed like I said something funny. "It doesn't feel so good to get shitted on, does it? You have been screwing Camille for lord knows how long, the lies, betrayal and not to forget how you messed up my life as well as our family!"

"Michelle, by sleeping with that low down Detective Floyd?"

"Greg, you don't even know him."

"So, you do after minutes of fucking?" I told her.

"Yes, those were the best minutes of my life!" She said, throwing things across the room.

As bad as it hurt me to see my wife caught in the act, I guess I deserved it. I knew she did it out of anger. I walked over to calm her down, but she pushed me away. I couldn't believe my marriage went from ten to zero in an instant. My wife cursed more, did things that were out of her character, but I guess if the tables were turned, I would be the same way.

Although what she did was foul, we really needed to talk. It was getting late and I was drained. I dialed Ed and apologized for what he saw. My marriage was just fucked up I told him. I ended the call, took a muscle relaxer, and headed to bed.

* * *

The morning after I was still sore, but glad to be in my own bed. I heard Michelle laughing on the phone and peeked in to see who she was talking to. She ignored me, so I walked out the room and headed for the shower.

Once in the shower I told myself I was getting my marriage back on track; I didn't care what happened last night, all I wanted was Michelle. Apparently, she heard my thoughts because she came in opened the shower door and got in, naked. She kissed me, but I was scared to touch her, I didn't know what was going on through her mind.

"You're not going to touch your wife?"

"Baby, I'm sorry, this was the last thing I expected."

She fondled me; I finally fondled back, caressed her breasts, and kissed her. I couldn't help but think back to the image in my head of her and the detective. Michelle on top of him made me cringe. She turned around and told me to enter her from the back. I did what she asked and it felt more like sex than us bonding. I couldn't get into it, but played it off. She made me sit in the shower chair and she straddled me, I watched my wife enjoy herself because I was having a hard time coping. She came, washed up, and disappeared, leaving me wondering what was next.

I went downstairs as Michelle got dressed and heard my phone ring. It was the care facility where Camille had been transported. She went to lock up but had a crazy spell so she ended up there. I was asked if I could visit her, for her to calm down, I told them, "Hell no!" but they insisted on one visit to see if they could use this as a session.

I immediately dialed Ed, and talked to him about it. He thought it wasn't a bad idea, this way it may prove if she's really sane or not. He said he would go down with me and that I didn't have to see her but five minutes. I agreed and hung up.

Michelle came around the corner, didn't say a word, and left out the door.

I threw on a pair of sweats and a t-shirt, and then waited for Ed. He was handling the business and I appreciated him for that. Ed picked me up and we went down to the facility, which was about an hour away. This gave me time to catch up with Ed. He thought Michelle was playing mind games to get even, but really thought I should bust a cap in Detective Floyd's ass. I'm just going to let it roll for now, but if it happened again, then I would. I told him it's different when your wife cheats; Ed said nothing was different about it, only she's a woman and I'm a man.

We arrived at this crazy place; Ed went to speak with the doctors. The District Attorney also arrived and was informed I was coming. He's still trying to prosecute Camille, or if that doesn't happen, then get her transported to a facility in Holbrook, Arizona, miles away from here. My skin started itching and I wasn't in any shape to deal with this woman.

The doctor came and explained to us the situation; that Camille thought we were married with a son and had been asking for me non-stop. She was having tantrums and throwing things, she just came out of a padded room where she was in a straight jacket for twenty-four hours. I couldn't believe I was here doing this, seeing the woman who messed up my life. I started having second thoughts; I turned to walk down the hall, then the doctor called my name.

I went into the room and was startled by what I saw: a frail Camille talking to herself in a corner holding a picture of me while I slept. I wondered where the hell she got that from. There's no telling what she did when I fell asleep at her place, I guess that's how she got my home number by rambling.

"Camille," I called out.

"Greg, baby, is that you?" she said, her eyes got big and she ran to me like a kid. "I knew you would come."

She tried to hug me and I told her that wasn't a good idea. She stepped back and asked about our son and what meal should she cook when she gets home. "Look, Greg, you remember this picture?" She pulled out a dozen pictures of me, most of them while I slept, naked, and a picture of me and her that she snapped including herself in it. Now, tell me that's not crazy!

"Camille, please have a seat," I said, which she did with no hesitation.

"What is it, Greg?"

I explained to her the situation and that she harmed my family...

"Greg, I did it for us! She said, "You love me, remember? Why did you say it?" she asked waiting on an answer.

"Camille, I don't know. I did care for you when we became friends, but that's all it was; I have a wife, remember?"

She was in denial about the whole thing, she started bringing up things we discussed, things I may have said but didn't mean, and she kept a journal of that including date and time. This thing was getting more sickening by the minute. I turned to leave but stopped and turned around to tell her to get over herself and that I know she's playing a game to keep from going to jail it's all an act.

She just smiled, "Greg, I will always love you. When I get out of here, we'll be together." Then she started to cry. Greg this, and Greg that, Greg Jr, our family, I had to leave. I called for the guard to let me out, she banged on the door like hell, hollering "Greg, Greg, come back!"

I shivered in the hallway. Her screams gave me chills. I turned around and saw Michelle come out with Ed and the doctors, and I was wondering what was she was doing here.

I greeted her, she said she overheard me on the phone earlier and decided to come down. She hugged me and all of a sudden we heard a "crash." Camille had thrown a chair against the door, breaking the window. She had a break down when Michelle hugged me. We looked on the monitors and she was going crazy. Camille grabbed a needle and tried to stick herself. A team of care members ran in and took the needle, sedated her, and put her back in a straight jacket. Lord knows I never saw that happen before.

I looked at Ed and said, "Maybe she isn't acting; no one goes through loops like that to stay out of jail, do they?"

"You'll be surprised," the District Attorney said.

The next step was to wait it out, but I needed to take every precaution for me and my family should this nut case break out of here.

I wasn't willing to go through this again!

Chapter 44

Camille

These doctors think I'm crazy, but maybe I really am and was just kidding myself. I started talking to myself more, itched really badly, and had tantrums for no reason.

When Greg came to visit me, I was so nice and thought he had left Michelle, and then she showed up after his visit and hugged him. That really threw me over the edge. When I get out of here, I am going to make her pay; she destroyed everything in my life. I thought by now she would have been out the picture for good.

I had hopes of me and Greg being together and him getting me out of this place. They had me in this straight jacket where I couldn't move. They had me taking all kinds of meds. I cried more and more each day. I was so alone I didn't know who to trust. First Walter, then Nikki, now Greg; they all betrayed me and were now gone from my life. But, I knew Greg would be back.

I thought about the life Walter and I once had. It was good until he cheated on me and wanted a divorce. I couldn't deal with him leaving me, so I had to act fast. Seeing him in that casket was confirmation that he would not be walking the streets with that tramp ever again. The psychiatrist walked in and interrupted my thoughts, and I was angry she did that. People were always fucking with me, why wouldn't they just let me be?

"Camille," the fat lady called out.

I looked at her and smiled. She started the session by asking me how I felt; did I feel like the medicine was working? Then she wanted to discuss my family history.

"Ms. Jean, I have no family, my mom died when I was young, I never knew my dad, and I moved from Memphis to North Carolina to be with my best friend, Nikki, when she got a job offer. So, I have no clue about my family; Greg is my family," I said calmly.

"Oh, I see," she said. "So, where is Nikki?"

"Dead! I didn't mean to kill her," I cried. I went on and on how she betrayed me and didn't want to see me happy. I sat there in a daze. "Why is everyone so concerned with Nikki? What about me?" I yelled at the lady.

Ms. Jean called out several times before I looked at her. "Walter and Greg both hurt me, I have no one to call mine; that was all I wanted. But no, they played me, used me, and took me for granted. Ms. Jean, what are you going to do about it? Huh?" I asked, waiting on an answer.

She hugged me, and then she whispered, "It's going to be okay, Camille."

She talked for a while about 'closure' and how to mentally overcome that, as well as my mental state. They were labeling me as bipolar with a schizoid personality disorder, which is a psychiatric condition with a lifelong pattern of indifference to others that disconnected me from reality. The more she talked, the more I tuned her out. It all went in one ear and out the other. I started singing and I got loud, not wanting to hear anymore of her bullshit.

Ms. Jean stood up, extended her hand, and when I didn't acknowledge her, she said she would see me on Friday. She signaled for the guard to open the door.

I was glad she was gone; she was ugly to look at anyway.

I looked around the room and it became smaller and smaller. I heard the door open and it was a nurse bringing my meds. She let me out of that jacket, took me to potty and to wash up, then after that I went to an area with a room full of people. They were all crazy! I didn't know if I'd rather be in here or in lock up.

I noticed security everywhere and monitors. I just knew I was going to escape this place. I would just have to give it time and come up with a plan to get out this hellhole. They had televisions, a game room, library, radio, and even a computer, but it could only be accessed by a personnel user.

I was computer smart so I would figure it out and send Greg an email. I grabbed the newspaper and sat on the couch with a lady talking to herself and pointing at the ceiling. I opened the paper and saw me and Greg in it.

"Look, look!" I pointed to the paper. "That's me you see?" I told the lady sitting beside me. "That's my husband!" I said beaming.

The lady laughed and continued to look at the ceiling; she nudged me in the side. "Is he coming to get you out of here?" she asked and laughed.

"Yes, soon I hope, real soon!"

I went to the front office and asked for scissors. I wanted to cut the pictures out the paper and put them on my wall. We weren't allowed to have scissors, knives, pens, or anything sharp for fear of harming ourselves. Only personnel were able to assist us with any of those items. The blonde lady got out scissors, took the paper, and I told her what to cut out. She did and I was happy.

I skipped to the television area, sat down with others, and watched the news and more stories of Greg and me all over. I told everyone in the room to look at me, that I was on TV. They all clapped, one guy said, "Hooray to the killer!" I turned around and snapped at him, giving him an evil look. "You bastard, you better hush, if you know what's good for you!"

The guy yelled at me from across the room, gave me the middle finger, flashed his ass, and then left the room.

I growled. I stared at my pictures, and then I kissed them; Greg would always be with me now. Although I missed my son, I knew they would both be back soon or I would go to them.

Chapter 45

Michelle

I woke up to the smell of breakfast. Carlos carried a tray into the bedroom filled with bacon, eggs, french toast, grits, and fresh fruits. I stayed at his place on the other side of town to get away from all the drama in my life. His place was nice and cozy and he didn't mind me staying at all.

I have stayed in contact with Carlos since the day Greg caught us together. Although I used him to hurt Greg. He was everything a woman wants in a man, but I didn't want a relationship with anyone, at least not right now.

Carlos looked at me while I ate and I was pleased that he knew how to cook. Carlos was sweet, understanding, and down to earth. He knew what we were doing was no strings attached and enjoyed every bit of it. We even went out a couple times far away from Atlanta since I was blasted all over the news and didn't want anyone to recognize me.

After I ate, we had sex again. He was a beast and I craved him. I never knew I would enjoy another man's touch. He had a little time left then he had to get ready for work. Afterwards I showered, put on my clothes, fixed my hair then applied some make-up. I had a meeting with the attorney I called earlier. We kissed, promised to get together soon, and I left him standing in the doorway.

I drove in the Atlanta traffic down 75 about 25 miles on the outskirts of Atlanta and reached the office of Claudia Vail. I walked in, signed in, and seated myself. I waited for about five minutes until she called me into her office.

"Michelle, it's finally nice to meet you," Claudia said as she greeted me.

"Thanks, it's a pleasure," I responded.

I took a seat in her lavish office. It was spacious and nicely decorated. Her décor was well put together from the colors, furniture, and the wall art. Whoever decorated this office was on point, I thought. I asked about her decorator and to my surprise, it was Camille Young! My expression changed quickly. "Camille had sense enough to decorate something," I mumbled. Claudia explained it was decorated over a year ago and personally she doesn't know Camille, her assistant referred her after she decorated a friend's home when she first got to Atlanta. That friend was Camille's first client, so there was nothing to be concerned about, she assured me.

I didn't know Camille was an interior decorator, but I really didn't know anything about her nor did I care.

Claudia admitted she followed my story in the press and knew all that I'd been through. Claudia had a great reputation and I called on her to handle my divorce because she was good at what she did. I didn't want anyone to feel sorry for me, but to learn from the ordeal. She asked about Greg and I told her he had no idea I was filing for divorce. He was thinking we could get past this, but I simply couldn't.

We went through a list of questionnaires, talked about counseling, and proceeded with a petition for divorce. I hoped Greg would agree with the settlement and let me go so this could be simple. We would have joint custody of our son, split the vacation property we shared, our savings, and the rest of the accounts we had together. I was willing to let him stay in the house because I didn't want to. I wanted a fresh start and found the perfect house in Florida close to Dianne. The meeting took about two hours, and I was glad I got through it. Claudia said Greg would be served and she would keep me posted.

I thanked her and was on my way out. I didn't want to be seen out that much, every time I went somewhere people recognized me from the news or newspaper. It was annoying. I stopped by Marlow's Tavern to grab something to eat and headed home. I drove in silence wondering how one could be so happy one day and so sad the next. I couldn't believe my marriage was over; it was all I could think about. I would be a single mother and that had never crossed my mind. Greg and I were supposed to raise our son together as a family. I wanted so badly to walk in the door and run into Greg's arms but I couldn't, the sex in the shower was nothing, I was losing myself in Greg's pit of a game. I wiped my tears as I drove into the garage.

I walked into the house and saw roses everywhere. Greg appeared behind me taking my hand and leading me to the table. He prepared food. Everything from oysters, steak, steamed vegetables, scallops, red dirty potatoes, and mango shrimp. I had to put my food I just ordered in the fridge. He prepared our meals, poured wine, and sat me down. I wanted so badly to tell him about the divorce, but didn't want to spoil his moment; I figured I'd go along with him until the shit hit the fan. The thought of him opening the envelope with the divorce papers would be priceless; I smiled, laughed, ate, and joked with Greg one last time.

Chapter 46

Greg

I woke up to my wife looking gorgeous as ever with no makeup on. She always looked good that way and especially in the nude. Sex last night was amazing. We Skyped Michelle's parents and saw Jr.; we baby talked with him and it was nice to see my son smiling and happy. He was getting bigger by the day. Hopefully he wouldn't be with them for that much longer.

"Hello beautiful," I said, when Michelle opened her eyes.

"Hi, you," she said, looking around, "What happened last night?"

"You know what happened, we did the-you-know-what," I said smiling.

She turned her head and was silent after that. I asked what's wrong and she responded, "That wasn't supposed to happen," she apologized, and stated we have a lot to discuss. I agreed and once we both got dressed, we could talk about everything and finally move forward.

I called into the office, checked in, and responded to some emails in the office downstairs. Ed called. We talked about the case in D.C. that was in progress and how it would be handled. I was still recovering and didn't want to risk over doing it, so I worked a little from home. I knew people were whispering at the office about me, but Ed never said anything. He just kept it professional. I was really embarrassed at what I did and the effect it had on my entire family. I knew what I did put a strain on the business and I thought about giving it all up, but needed something to keep me busy. I thanked Ed daily for handling things while I was away and appreciated his hard work. He was the one person that didn't judge me. He advised me and always told me the truth, but never once judged me. My family was just like his family so he understood what I put everyone through.

I heard Michelle in the kitchen, as I walked out the office to see if she wanted anything to eat. She had her back turned and was texting someone on her cell phone; Michelle stated she wasn't hungry. As Michelle left the room, leaving her phone on the counter, it vibrated; curious I picked it up and saw a text message from Detective Floyd a.k.a Carlos. I was at a loss for words because I thought it was a onetime thing – her using him to get back at me. Michelle walked back in the kitchen and immediately took her phone out my hand.

"What the hell do you think you're doing?" she said defensively.

"You're still seeing that no good detective?"

"I am what is it to you?"

"Michelle, babe, come on. Why do we keep hurting each other? We've already been through so much," I said pleading with her.

"We wouldn't even be at this place in our lives if it wasn't for you!"

At that point I knew we had to talk right then and there. I took her by the hands and sat her down on the couch. Before I could sit down the doorbell rang, I looked at the monitor, and saw it was a courier. I opened the door, the gentlemen stated he had a package for a Greg Langston, I signed for it and he said, "You've been served, sir," and walked off. I was curious and clueless at the same time so I opened the package and what I saw and read confused me. Divorce papers from Michelle Langston! My wife!

I walked back to the living room area in shock. She looked at me and asked, "Who was it?" I tossed the package on the couch next to her.

"So, you want a divorce?" I asked, "And when were you planning on telling me?" I yelled, feeling like a fool.

"Yes, Greg, I want a divorce. I was planning on telling you last night."

"When during sex? Or after you've made a complete fool of me?" I fired back.

"I can't live like this anymore…the lies, betrayal, the cheating, and let's not forget putting this entire family in danger. I can't move on like nothing happened, I just can't do it! Greg, I saw how you looked at Camille at the facility and you mentioned to her you once loved and cared for her when she asked you did you ever. How can I compete with that lunatic? You caught feelings for your mistress? Wasn't I enough Greg? Wasn't I! I was a damn good wife, Greg! While I'm thinking you're working late you're at her house serving her up while I'm sitting here preparing your meals, so you don't think I want a divorce? You damn right I do!" Michelle said.

Michelle went on and on in anger so deep that she got up in my face in tears. She had the same questions that I didn't have answers to. Yes, I admitted I screwed up; it didn't have anything to do with her. I was very happy with Michelle the reason I cheated was something I couldn't answer. I love Michelle with all of me and was hoping we could get past this, but if the shoe were on the other foot, could I forgive her so easily and move on? I thought about it and knew I couldn't.

I listened to Michelle, I even pleaded with her for a second chance, but that wasn't enough, I hurt her way too badly. I didn't want to think about seeing my child on the weekends, holidays, and being a part time father. I always thought we would raise our kids together and it could have been that way, if I hadn't screwed it up.

I picked up the envelope, looked at Michelle, and went into the office. I cried at the thought of being alone, losing my family, and starting over.

There I spent that day – one of many – alone and depressed.

Chapter 47

Ed

I received so much backlash from Greg's press in the news that it had taken a toll on me and the firm. People didn't want to do business with us. The business declined by thirty percent; although, we had a great reputation and great attorneys, it was hard trying to bounce back.

I had to take on the extra clients Greg dealt with before his situation exploded in the news, and delegated the others to our new attorney, Mark.

Mark was great; a graduate from Howard University. His background was interesting and he worked on some very important cases and won them all. He moved to Atlanta months ago with his wife and daughters and had several offers, but chose to work for our firm. Hopefully we will make him partner soon because he was a blessing. The clients thought that Greg's personal life would put a strain on their case that he actually didn't have time for them. I understood from a client perspective what they were feeling.

As a friend and partner I touched base with Greg daily, I handled the business on a professional level, and helped him as an attorney. Greg's problems had also become my problems. I wished he would have stopped seeing Camille a long time ago when I told him she had screws loose.

Michelle was like a sister to me and she was really hurting. She has come to me several times, but I didn't let Greg know that. I handled him on one level and Michelle on another. Michelle was very vulnerable and weak; she was saying things she would never say. I gave her the best advice I could and told her to do what's best for her and Jr. I let her know that I would always be there for the both of them. Before she left, she kissed me and walked off.

I learned that Camille was being held responsible for Walter and Nikki's murders, kidnapping charges, endangering a child, attempted murder for Michelle, and weapons charges, but instead of jail she's being transported to Arizona.

"Ain't that some shit?" I told the District Attorney. He fought hard on the case; a judge ruled her incompetent with all kinds of mental disorders and said she would not survive in jail. Given that Walter and Nikki didn't survive, I could care less if she did. The facility was to stay in contact with Greg and Michelle on any changes about whether Camille was being transferred, her whereabouts at all times, even if an escape has taken place; this allows them to protect themselves at all times.

I notified Greg of Camille's case and although he wasn't pleased, he was glad she was far away from Atlanta and still on lock down. He told me Michelle asked for a divorce and was moving with Jr. in a couple of weeks. I could tell in his voice he had being crying, sad, and depressed. I tried to lift his spirits, but he just said, he'd holler at me later.

I hung up with Greg and contacted Michelle. She was pleased at the outcome, but like Greg, she wished Camille was in jail. I talked to her about her plans, she promised to stay in touch. She wanted to get out of Atlanta and start over fresh and I could understand that. She said she would always love Greg and, who knows, you can never tell what the future holds.

I ended the call to a knock on my door and it was Claudia Vail, a respected attorney who has been in business for years. Not sure why she was here, but she came in and bluntly asked, "Would it be feasible to buy Greg Langston out of his half of the business?" Shocked at what she was up to, but curious to know and pick her brain, I told her to have a seat.

Chapter 48

Greg

The days just passed me by. Ever since the day I was served with those divorce papers, I had been in a slump. I wanted so desperately for my marriage to work. I really didn't want to give Michelle a divorce. I've neglected answering my phone calls, emails, or eating. Michelle was off doing her own thing and has become this woman I had made her to be. I loved my wife so much; she could do whatever she liked if she wouldn't go through with the divorce.

I prayed daily, but one thing I did do was reach out to my pastor. Although I hadn't been to church in months, it was really embarrassing to start now. I was really scared to step foot back in a church because of how people viewed me now from the news and press. It was heartbreaking. Pastor Dennis came over and prayed with me, read scriptures, and talked about forgiving and how to move on. I was very interested in *Acts 3:19* as it read: *"Repent, then, and turn to God, so that your sins may be wiped out, that times of refreshing may come from the Lord,"* I opened my bible, which I hadn't done in a very long time, and engaged *Psalms 71:20-21*: *"You who have made me see many troubles and calamities will revive me again; from the depths of the earth you will bring me up again. You will increase my greatness and comfort me again."* Reading the bible has now become a daily ritual in my life.

I had been thinking about moving lately and selling my shares of the business to Ed. Like Michelle, I, too, needed a new start. I could always start my own practice somewhere else or venture out to something new. Michelle walked in and I spoke to her, she spoke back and it was very dry. I asked Michelle if we could talk for a moment, she agreed that was feasible. I kneeled down before her, apologized again, and asked her to please forgive me. I had been trying to renew myself to keep from being depressed, that I knew I had to let her go, so she could get on with her life even if it hurt me.

I talked to Michelle about being a good wife and that she was as *Proverbs 18:22* states, *"He who finds a wife finds a good thing and obtains favor from the Lord."* What I didn't do was obtain favor from the Lord and if I did, I wouldn't be granting her the divorce she asked for. I asked Michelle again was she sure and she looked at me and said "yes." I understood and had to let her be free of me. I couldn't sit and worry about if she was still sleeping with Detective Floyd because I pushed her into him arms.

"Greg, I notice the change in you and it's a start," she said. "I just wish you had this urge a year ago and we wouldn't be standing here now."

Michelle told me she loved me and always will, we have a bond and that's Jr. I told her I was seriously thinking about selling my shares of the business and moving on. I knew my problems were weighing on Ed and he had been catching hell from my absence. Ed has been a loyal friend and I do owe him that – to walk away. That way the business could regroup and bounce back from this storm I caused.

I wanted to ask Michelle about what she thought of me moving to Florida to be close to our son and that way she won't have to do everything on her own, but decided to save that question for another day. Michelle reached out her arms to me and we embraced. It felt good that she was getting past this and could find closure in it all. A crazy lunatic tormented my life; she looked precious as a diamond, but I've learned the hard way looks are deceiving.

Camille wrote me several times and I had to contact the facility in Arizona to put a stop to all that. I haven't received a letter in weeks now. I did pray for her; she was the most damaged of us all. Ed located a brother of hers she hasn't spoken to or seen in years. He thought she was dead. With no other family members, her brother had started visiting her, so that was great news. I cleared my thoughts, grabbed the documents, and gave the signed copies to Michelle. "Thanks, Greg," she said, smiled, and walked off.

The doorbell rang and she exited; I went to answer it and behold, it was Detective Floyd.

"Hello, Greg," he said.

"'Sup," was all I said. Any other day I would whip his ass for coming to my house like this, but I figured Michelle was no longer mine, but what I did do was slam the door in his face and called out for Michelle. I told her that her boyfriend was outside.

Michelle came down the hall, "Who?" she said, after looking out the window. "Greg, are you jealous?"

"Hell, yeah, I am, but I have no right to be," I said and walked off.

She stood outside the door for about ten minutes and came back in with a gift box, curiously, I just looked on. My soon to be ex-wife was enjoying her freedom at my expense and I was burning deep down inside.

Chapter 49

Michelle

Moving day had almost arrived and I packed most of my things to have shipped to Dianne's place for storage. I had plans to interview once I got there and got situated; that way I can find the perfect nanny for the baby.

Greg was enjoying the baby ever since he had returned home. Greg Jr. was now six months old and the happiest baby ever. His smile beamed every time I saw him. My life was starting to pick back up and I felt happier than I had ever been. My dad was glad I was divorcing Greg, a process that should be final soon. "A man that puts you and your family in danger is no good for you," my dad said to me. The thing my father wouldn't like was that Greg was also moving to Florida, not with me, but to be close to us for the baby's sake. I really thought that was a great idea, this way he can start over as well.

We both went to church on Sunday with the baby and as awkward as it was, it felt good to be in the house of the Lord. I got up and spoke because I had a testimony. I also told Greg I forgive him in front of the congregation, because if I didn't, I wouldn't be able to move on.

The members of the congregation were so proud of us. Pastor Dennis' sermon spoke on *Luke 6:37*, which read: *'Judge not, and you will not be judged; condemn not, and you will not be condemned; forgive, and you will be forgiven.'*

That passage spoke to us all and I was glad that no one judged Greg on the bad decision he made. After service we went into the Pastor's office and talked to him briefly and told him of our plans to move to Florida. He was sad, but totally understood and wished us both the best and we promised to stay in contact.

Greg seemed happy as well, I think the baby made a big impact on him. Greg was also meeting with Ed and an attorney with a public notary to sign over his shares of the business and for Ed to buy him out and move Claudia Vail in. Although Greg didn't care, I just found it strange that all of a sudden Ms. Vail was partnering with Ed at Langston. It wasn't my business so I didn't push the issue or complain about it. I was moving that weekend and Greg was coming down next weekend. He found a cozy condo on the beach that I thought was perfect for when the baby came over.

Dianne didn't like the idea that Greg was making his way back into my life, but I told her it would help me out and that I was leaving the past behind me, as well as Greg. I was not going back!

Carlos dropped by to hand me another gift and told me not to open it until I got to Florida. He promised to visit soon. He was a good guy, but under the circumstances timing was bad.

What Greg didn't know was that I retrieved all letters Camille wrote him and the last letter she wrote she promised to be out soon so they could be together. What I didn't understand was how a woman could make a man want her. It just took me back to that awful day when I got my son back from that crazy lady. A woman's instinct is always right; I just knew she had him, I just knew. What I did do was put a stop to the letters because somehow they kept coming even when I overheard Greg call the facility to have them stopped.

Breaking away from my thoughts, I promised Dianne a girl's night out when I got there. I was long overdue for a stiff drink and maybe I could have a one night stand, I laughed out loud. When I mean starting over, I mean starting over, from my head to my feet. "Maybe the single life won't be too bad after all," I thought.

I heard my phone vibrating and saw it was Ed. I answered it. He called to apologize for the kiss, which I tried to put out of my mind, but the last time I was at his office to see him telling him of my plans, as I was about to leave, he grabbed my arm and kissed me. Instead of pushing him away, I kissed him back. Not sure if he thought I was vulnerable or what, so I just left and didn't bring it up again. I told him I didn't understand why he kissed me, but accepted his apology. He wished me luck and I blurted, "By the way Ed, I hope that kiss was all you dreamed of," and hung up.

I jumped and was startled to find Greg standing behind me.

"What the hell is going on, Michelle? Is Ed kissing up on you now?" Greg said, waiting on an answer.

"Greg, it wasn't like that!" I said trying to explain to him the best way I could, but I didn't have an answer myself on why Ed kissed me, I simply told him it's in the past and it was nothing.

"Like hell it is," Greg said and stormed off.

Epilogue

Camille

I had the craziest dream again, but this time it was a good dream. In it I was happy, very happy and in my right frame of mind. I had this wonderful husband who just loved me for me and adored the ground I walked on. In my dream I also had a son and a daughter I was able to conceive. The life in my dream was all I ever wanted in real life.

I lived in this big house filled with warm colors such as yellow, sage, red, orange, and gold. My kids had this big yard to play in and it was the greatest feeling ever to be surrounded by love and those of your own.

My husband and I had regular dates, he brought me flowers just because, and I was the love of his life. In this dream, I was with my own man and he belonged to me. Not Mary Stevenson or Michelle, but mine. I've always been second best, but this time I was first place and it felt damn good to be loved.

I enjoyed family time, we would all get together on Friday nights and play Scrabble, Twister, eat pizza, pop popcorn, and watch a movie. When everyone fell asleep, I looked at them all, kissed them, and thanked God for my precious jewels. This was what having a family feels like. I cherished every moment of waking up to these people God had placed in my life.

When I needed someone to talk to, Nikki was always there for me and she was my kids' godmother. We would have lunch on the weekend, go shopping, and get pampered starting at the spa. Nikki would remind me of how good of a friend, mother, and wife I was, especially when I seemed to doubt myself. She was the ying to my yang, and I have never trusted anyone the way I do Nikki. She was always someone I could count on for anything and I always valued her opinion.

Also in my dream I'm a successful decorator and have been called on by many of Atlanta's finest celebrities from Ludacris, to Mychael Knight.

One of my projects was also featured in one of Tyler Perry's film. I was making a great life for myself and my husband was also successful as an entertainment attorney representing those of T.I. to Usher. We both had it going on I must admit.

I didn't have a relationship with my family and I was at peace with that, but I did contact my brother I haven't seen in ages and we finally reconnected. He knew I would be successful somewhere behind the scene. He knew I had that drive and determination in me.

Sometimes, I will have evil dreams such as the one with Taj and Mary and I welcome them, but not all dreams are the same, but my good dreams I recall the most. The good dreams will help me hold on to hope and that one day I'll be married with kids even if I have to adopt them. I'll get my mind together mentally, get released on good behavior, and start a new life somewhere. I realized that I can be happy, but it had to start within and in order to do so, I had to admit to having a problem and get help. I have the opportunity of starting over if I can overcome my past life.

I will always be haunted by the people I hurt – Walter, Nikki, Greg Jr., Michelle, and even Greg. Maybe they can forgive me for my sins and learn to get past the past. I hope one day I can trade my crazy personality in for the good one for good, and hopefully my dreams will be forever sweet and also lived out.

Acknowledgments

First and foremost I would like to give honor to my Heavenly Father, who made all of this possible. Thank you, Lord for guiding me through this book, my life and for the many blessings.

I could not have done this without the love and the support of my family. My husband and kids: Edward, Jada, Hunter, & Chayse…I love you all unconditionally!

Thanks to Octavia Sims for anything that I asked of you. You did it with no hesitation. Love you girl! Additionally, supporters: Keisha Thornton, Chatauna Nevels, and Bre Watson. Editor Perri Forrest, thank you as well!

Also I would like to thank my entire family, friends, readers, blogs, bookclubs, and bookstores for your support.

Ya girl,
Bianca

Readers Club Guide:

SOMEONE TO CALL MY OWN

by Bianca

1. Would you be willing to jump through hoops to be with someone, who's already taken?

2. Was Greg wrong for stringing Camille along knowing he had no intentions on being with her? Do you think he deserved what happened in the outcome?

3. Do you think it was wise of Michelle to take matters into her own hands? Why or why not?

4. What would you do, knowing you have been right all along regarding your mate's partner?

5. Do you really think Camille was insane or using that as an escape to not go to jail? Why or why not?

6. Was Michelle wrong for sleeping with Detective Floyd? What do you think her reasoning was behind it (anger, hurt, pain) or all of the above?

7. Could Nikki have done more to help the situation and Camille?

8. Knowing what Camille might have been capable of, how do you think Greg handled the situation with her?

9. Who do you think kissed who first (Michelle or Ed)?

10.   As a mother what would you have done to bring your baby back safely?

Thanks to all the book clubs, fans and most of all purchasing and reading "Someone To Call My Own." It was my pleasure to bring these characters to life!

OTHER BOOKS by BIANCA HARRISON

Forever His Wife

Inseparable

Deliver Me From Temptation

Deliver Me From Temptation 2

All books can be found on the Author Amazon Page:

amazon.com/author/biancaharrison

Follow the Author:

https://www.facebook.com/authorbiancaharrison

https://twitter.com/mrsjanielle

Instagram/mrsjanielle

Snapchat/mrsjanielle

Bianca is also available for book discussions, book signings, talks, and workshops. Please email her at authorbiancaharrison@gmail.com.

Made in the USA
Columbia, SC
19 July 2019